THE DREAM ANTILLES

THE DREAM ANTILLES

David Seth Michaels

iUniverse, Inc.

New York Lincoln Shanghai

The Dream Antilles

iUniverse books may be ordered through booksellers or by contacting:

iUniverse
2021 Pine Lake Road, Suite 100
Lincoln, NE 68512
www.iuniverse.com
1-800-Authors (1-800-288-4677)

ISBN-13: 978-0-595-35785-7 (pbk)
ISBN-13: 978-0-595-80254-8 (ebk)
ISBN-10: 0-595-35785-7 (pbk)
ISBN-10: 0-595-80254-0 (ebk)

Printed in the United States of America

For Ona
with love and gratitude

Don't wait any longer.

Dive
in
the ocean,
Leave
and let the sea
be you.

Silent, absent,
walking
an empty road,

all praise.

-Rumi[*]

*.   Coleman Barks & Michael Green, The Illuminated Rumi (1997, Broadway Books), p. 59

CHAPTER 1

▼

Oscar Sanchez, Jr., was the first person born in desde Desdemona and is its oldest native. He was born in the sea near the tree house he now occupies.

His parents, who were members of what passed in coastal Guyana for the Capulet and Montague families, ran away when they discovered that his mother was pregnant. Their departure was so urgent that it did not seem to matter that they had failed to decide on a destination. They filled a dugout with every possible item they thought might be essential to create a new life somewhere on an island, pointed the dugout toward the open sea, watched the coastline recede in the distance, and sighed relief that they were alone together and out of sight of the shore.

They were sure nobody could pursue them or find them. Said Oscar, Sr., in his most hopeful voice, "There are probably lots of islands in the sea nearby."

But, of course, none of them appeared. After four days, when all their food was gone and only a thimble full of water remained, they sat staring at the horizon, watching its gentle rise and fall, wondering if theirs had been too impulsive an idea. Despair, which stalked their voyage across the ocean, was ready to climb into the boat and pounce on them. It was held at bay only by the intensity of their gratitude for being together.

As the fourth sun set on the soon to be very parched couple, a pod of dolphins arrived. The biggest dolphin began to push the dugout around in a large circle and to whistle. The others jumped and frolicked nearby. Amazed and delighted at this omen, Oscar for reasons he could not later explain, jumped into the sea toward the dolphins. It was as if he were trying to solicit their help in finding land. In the emerging desperation, this jump seemed logical.

As soon as Oscar hit the water, however, the biggest dolphin surprised him with an extremely passionate, very aquatic embrace. Oscar was amazed and extremely excited. He was even more amazed when after just a few minutes of the caress he was tossed gently back into the dugout. There, he discovered a message had lodged in his mind. It was an understanding, a fact. It was incontestable. The dolphins would now transport them to a lovely, unoccupied island; they could relax. All was well after all. They would see it was so before long.

The dugout wallowed in the sea all night long. All night Oscar and Milagros slept fitfully, awakening because of thirst and hunger, going back to sleep after finding neither food nor drink nor an island had emerged. In his dreams Oscar was fishing on a turqoise sea and talking with the other fishermen in his boat. But whenever he moved to pull in the net or adjust his line or to drink from a flask, he awoke to find Milagros lying against the gunwales, to see only the bright canopy of stars overhead and to feel the gentle roll of the dugout as it slid on the swell. Where were they going? How long would it take to get there?

In the early morning, as the tide fell and the predawn light turned the horizon pink, the dugout was grounded on what initially appeared to be a postage stamp sized beach on the island of desde Desdemona. The dolphins were nowhere to be found.

Oscar and his beloved watched the tide slowly recede and a huge, flat, white sand beach emerge. They climbed trees, ate coconuts and mangoes and papayas, and rejoiced in each others' arms. Their celebration was terminated several hours later by their noticing that the tide was returning and that it would overrun the island and again completely submerge the beach. Oscar laughed out loud, hitting his open palm on his forehead, "Ai! Mi amor, we must tie up the boat and take to the trees. Those dolphins have some sense of humor. It's just a monkey island! And we must now become its monkeys."

*   *   *   *

There is a question whether desde Desdemona is an intermittent island or a sandbar with trees, or both, or neither. One thing is certain: twice a day at high tide the sea covers everything except the two large rocks that mark the ends of the reef, and the trees, which hold the tree houses and catwalks that make up desde Desdemona's villages. At low tide, the villages are joined by a very broad, very flat white sand beach.

Nearly 200 families live full or part time on desde Desdemona. The most recent waves of families arrived in the mid-1980s and late 1990s. In the 80s they were mostly investment bankers who had cashed out; in the 90s, Internet capital-ists. Previous waves included hippies and spiritual searchers. All now make their living either from passive income generated in their past incarnations or from desde Desdemona's main industry, limited tourism. Very little is required to thrive. In most circumstances wearing a t-shirt makes one over dressed. There are no signs declining service to those without shoes.

There is only one way to visit desde Desdemona: by invitation. The entire package is $600 per day per person or $400 per week per family or something in between. The rates are a complete mystery. And it must always take at least two full days of travel from everywhere to reach the island.

The currency in desde Desdemona is the *sonrise*. The bills are the colors of the rainbow, from red through indigo in ascending denominations. Somewhere on each bill is a dolphin, a local fruit, and a dugout canoe. One *sonrise* is worth about 1 US dollar. Because the limited tourism program provides all a guest can eat or drink, and because all activities are free, visitors spend money only on sou-venirs and whatever they may have forgotten to bring with them. "Locals," as they call themselves, speak English and Spanish and Spanglish and are willing to negotiate a deal on anything they have. They put items on sale primarily to create conversations. The obligatory haggling and trying on and discussing is just for fun, or to pass time, or to flatter or flirt. Or to gather news or reap opinions. It's just what's called "limin'" in the Southern Caribbean.

The slow process of purchasing emphasizes that each minute in desde Desde-mona still has 60 full seconds to enjoy, unlike New York or Chicago, which unbeknownst to their occupants, now have 44 and 48 seconds per minute, respectively. Selling things in desde Desdemona, much like the rest of life there, is just for fun.

The cuisine of desde Desdemona owes its debt not only to Milagros and Oscar Sanchez, but also to more recent arrivals. The national dishes are ceviche, which mixes Oscar's frequent catch of black snapper with Milagros's imported lime trees, and barbecued fish with mango chutney, which pays spicy homage to the ashram that appeared mid-island a few years after Oscar and Milagros.

There are dozens of kinds of fruit juice available, including guayaba and mora, and tourists find an ample supply of beer (usually Caribe or Red Stripe or Corona) and of California Chardonnay. The Chardonnay began appearing on the island in 1984 when a certain investment banker began to build a tree house for his family. As the result of some sort of inexplicable multi level marketing scheme, more and more arrives each year without cost and without being ordered. Locals, who originally loved such extravagant wine, now reserve it for tourists, preferring instead clear heads and bottled water. Most tourists rejoice at the Amazon like flow of grape.

*   *   *   *

The Milarepa Barbershop gives only one kind of haircut. The barber takes out the electric shaver, sets it on 4, and removes all but a uniform stubble. The only sound is the buzzing. It takes a while, because she is patient and tries to focus on her task. As Ona cuts, she tries to repeat to herself, "I am now cutting hair. My tool is sharp and easily makes heads smooth." She tries to focus on her breath, on the beating of her heart. But she is distracted. Bardo's mind wanders, too, to the Taoist story of the butcher who never needs to sharpen his knife because he is so thoroughly acquainted with how oxen are held together. He wonders about how cutting hair could be like that, and whether cutting the hairs one at a time with a tiny scissors would be more spiritual. He wonders how the hairs could be glued back on someone's head. He wonders why hair cutting is deemed low caste. But he, too, is distracted.

The ceremony Ona is performing, a ritual seemingly invented on the spot by Bardo and not really comprehensible, is in preparation for his fiftieth birthday. It releases a flood of questions and random thoughts. Ona becomes so absorbed in memories and remembrances about their 25 years of relationship, how it is living with him, loving him, having children with him, growing a family with him, how Bardo got there, and how at 50 he compares to his youthful 25 years, that she presses down too hard. The shaver responds by cutting a gouge through his hair to his scalp like a four lane interstate highway crossing a pine barren. The barber stifles her laughs as she returns to the haircut; the patron doesn't. Bardo frowns, touches the streak at the top of his head, squints at the mirror, and sighs.

If the patron paid for his haircuts, his complaints might have a place. But the Milarepa Barbershop is no ordinary unisex salon. Quite the contrary. It isn't a barbershop at all. It's in Bardo's mind. It's a single, wooden chair on a deck in a tree house overlooking the island of desde Desdemona, and Bardo will be its only patron this week.

The opening of the highway has brought Bardo back to the situation at hand. He again briefly ponders complaining. But complaining about this haircut will not remove the scrape. And, he observes, it would flirt with what enlightened people might call "demonstrating an egregious lack of equanimity." Bardo cherishes his equanimity and is proud to display it. Does some unseen teacher invite the barber to make gouges to test him? Or does the barber do it on her own? Or is it karma? Is it a veiled message from the universe speaking to them? Or is there no juice to be extracted from it, like squeezing a dried apricot in your fist. His search for understanding comes up with nothing.

He's not surprised by this. Bardo's next thoughts are of a story told about Gurdjieff. One devotee was obnoxious and a constant source of aggravation to the others. Ultimately, the others managed to berate him until he left. When he heard that this particular student had left, Gurdjieff himself went after him in a long, black limousine, and brought him back. It turned out that Gurdjieff had paid this disciple to be obnoxious and to aggravate the others.

Bardo knows after 25 years with her that nobody is paying this barber. Nobody has to. It's built in. Their relationship is constantly providing both delight and opportunities to both of them for the expansion of their individual humility. Most of these opportunities are gentle. He is pleased when he remembers this. They are lucky. The thought is comforting. He notes in passing that there are times when, trapped in events, he cannot remember the luckiness or the gentleness at all. He shakes his head at the idea of forgetting, trying somehow to embed this remembrance, to make it always accessible. Remembering he is lucky is surely a balm.

As he stands in front of the mirror, Bardo is surprised. His long, curly, salt and pepper fox terrier hair is gone. Instead, his head is covered with a stubble with the length and texture of a four day beard. His eyebrows look bushier. His forehead is the size of South Dakota. And there's an interstate highway across the top of his head aimed for Canada. All he needs are some micro machine cars, and some white-out to paint a center line. He rubs the palm of his hand across the highway.

The buzzing stops. This is what he has wanted. He can again hear the birds and the sea breaking on the beach below him.

"Ona, what about the rest?" he insists. His voice begins too loud. "I want all of it taken off to my waist. It's for my birthday. My fiftieth birthday. I came onto the planet with nothing, so I should start the second half with nothing also." She shrugs at this explanation, turns the buzzer back on, removes the chain guard, and begins to scrape across his shoulders. It is in preparation for his 50th birthday, she thinks. What on earth is he doing this for? She liked his long, curly, wild hair. She remembers the wild curls of his youth. He looks like a cop, or a skinhead, or a storm trooper, she thinks, and she doesn't like that at all. She will say nothing about it for now.

He smiles faintly. The second half is what it's about, he hypothesizes. The second half is decisive in the game. The first half culminates in the second half. The second half decides all the issues. He smiles at his cleverness, at his wonderful strategy for meeting the starting buzzer for the second half until his skin starts to chafe and redden. Then he turns directly to distraction, thinking about how exquisite sex will be when he is hairless and vulnerable and smooth, how her skin will feel across his smooth chest, her breath on his smooth shoulders. How making love with her like this will be a treasured event oft remembered. This train of thought, one he has carried with full intensity from its initial spark for twenty-five years, is hurtling off a trestle: in the mirror he sees her frowning at his back. She anticipates a problem. There is already ample chafing. Rawness. She does not consider it a hint of the erotic. She is thinking about how the sun will broil and desiccate his chafed hide, how he will complain. How he will complain and feel sorry for himself and perhaps even mope. How long will that go on?

She remembers the agony of his first, all over sun burn, some twenty-five years before and how he could not lie down and how he alternated between freezing and overheating. And how incessantly he complained. That was funny in retrospect; it could have been even funnier if there were some relief from the pain other than elapsing time.

He realizes above the drone of the buzzing that his shoulders and back hurt in a sharp, but familiar way. It's exciting and erotic, he thinks, overriding emerging thoughts that he's just stupid. Maybe, he allows, it's not such a great idea to cut all of this off. I wanted something dramatic, something creative for the second half. Something commemorative. Something to mark the event in a palpable way. It's all of that, but, then again, time will tell. There is a gnawing, repetitive thought that there must be a purpose for body hair, and that his removing it may cause him unforeseen, possibly dreadful problems. This too he fends away. Ona turns off the buzzing. She confirms his analysis, "I think this is going to hurt even more if you go in the sun. I don't see how you can avoid that living here."

He stares at the turquoise, glinting sea, the yellow sea plane bobbing at anchor, the tops of the palm trees, and the waves gently breaking on the reef that runs from the rocky headland in front of the deep water. He can hear children laughing and shouting in the distance. Somebody is snorkeling near the reef. He can feel the smooth roughness of his shoulders. He can feel the tropical sun beginning to barbecue his neck and back. "Thanks," he tells her as he pushes the Brillo hair from his lap and legs onto the floor. He stands at the railing looking at the sea, mixing excitement at his nakedness with emerging regret and dread. Then he wanders slowly down the catwalk, thinking about his skin, seeking new insights, seeing what's changed. No insights have arrived. So he continues to try to distract himself, "I didn't tell her how exquisite making love will be for us both."

Bardo shifts gears to thoughts of gratitude. The distraction is not working. He needs a reliable remedy, one that has always worked for him. He is thankful for his home, thankful for his family, thankful for the sun. It is an exercise he performs frequently. Today he is most thankful that desde Desdemona has become a home for him. He savors the feeling of gratitude for home as he descends the catwalk.

Ona seizes the broom and pushes the hair off the deck into the sea below. The lack of buzzing makes her thoughts much louder. She thinks, "At 50 Bardo's essentially the same as he was at 25 even though he's much different." She enjoys the contradiction. "We've been together now as long as he was in his life without me. For a milestone, a ceremony, his skin is going to hurt. I hope it's worth it to him. I don't get it." She watches a pelican land in the tree, and watches the branch bob up and down. "Is this an Old Testament idea, to make him holy? What's gotten into him?"

She picks out a mango, and starts to peal it. It is perfectly ripe. The smell of mango fills the air as its juice drips down her hands to her wrists. She remembers her first mangos, as a small child, picking them from her grandmother's trees on desde Desdemona, and her delight at their sticky sweetness. And she thinks about the community of round, black seeds, huddled together in a papaya, how they are joined by proximity and the thinnest of membranes. The papaya reminds her of desde Desdemona, their home.

*   *   *   *

Milagros Sanchez, Oscar's beloved, was a radiant beauty. It was her smile for which the currency in desde Desdemona was named. In March, 1929, a photograph of her standing on the beach, bare breasted, wrapped in a batik cloth, with her hands on her hips, appeared in a US travel magazine. The caption explained that paradise had been discovered in the Caribbean and that the exotic people of desde Desdemona were friendly and very beautiful. To no one's surprise, interest in desde Desdemona and its occupants was immediate. Yachts began to appear off shore. There were rumors of cruise ships, of mass immigration from nearby countries. Locals, all of whom understood exactly how beautiful Milagros was and how very powerful her attraction could be, immediately recognized that desde Desdemona was in the gravest danger. Desde Desdemona simply could not support the sudden interest and an influx of too many tourists would render the tree houses and the fragile beaches uninhabitable.

A hastily called meeting of the approximately 30 locals then residing on the island resulted in the first department in desde Desdemona's first de facto government: the Ministry of Limited Tourism. Its mission, quite simply, was to get desde Desdemona off the maps and out of the public eye. William Jameson, a retired railroad magnate with a reputation for stealth, intensity, and luck, was selected to be the first Minister. His plan of posting the waters surrounding the island with markers indicating sand bars and a quarantine was met half way in October, 1929, by the stock market crash. Within months the incipient interest in desde Desdemona was eclipsed by other events. Desde Desdemona was again a floating monkey island, an unthinkable, if not utterly forgotten destination.

*   *   *   *

Milagros's beauty was not her sole gift. Milagros's family had passed down from generation to generation the gift of knowledge of the healing qualities and energies of plants. Milagros, beginning as a tiny child, had learned from her grandmother the special crafts of healing with herbs and by touch. As she grew up, she learned every plant and tree and moss and all of the properties of each, and she knew how to prepare the plants so that fractured bones would mend, lacerations would heal, broken hearts would find peace and comfort, grief and fear would be dispelled, and a million other deep healing miracles could transpire. She continued the dialogue with the plant world begun by her grandmother in Guayana.

Because desde Desdemona was twice a day submerged, its native plant life was not sufficiently diverse for Milagros's purposes. She knew from the beginning that more, much more would be required than grew on desde Desdemona. She and Oscar built their first tree house with a palm leaf roof and bamboo gutters, and barrels to catch the rain, and a long series of planters and boxes to hold the earth. Eventually, Milagros began to make journeys to nearby islands to bring important plants and rich earth back to desde Desdemona. These voyages, taking up to four days round trip, brought to Milagros the plants she thought were essential for childbirth, for raising children, to heal any ailments she and her husband might develop, and for first aid. First Milagros developed the healing plants. Then she brought plants with beautiful flowers or delicious fruits or other qualities she admired. She brought fruit trees that were not indigenous to desde Desdemona. By the time she was ready to deliver her second child, Rosalita, Milagros and Oscar were living in comfort in what they called Eden del Caribe. They could easily feed themselves a variety of meals completely from their gardens and from the sea. And the air of desde Desdemona was enriched with the rich fragrance of an orderly succession of hundreds of blooms.

*   *   *   *

As he stood completely shorn on the beach, Bardo's slightly desperate press for more gratitude continued. In the waves, he could see that the glinting sea around desde Desdemona was filled with stories. Stories in ancient languages. Stories from Atlantis. Stories in English and Spanish and now forgotten languages of the original dwellers of the Caribbean. The stories were floating and drifting and touching each other. Some were complete; others were only fragments. Some were elaborate, complicated structures that wove themselves into gorgeous fabrics. Others were bare and had tattered holes in them. Some were tiny jewels; others, just blotches in the sea. Some stories were made up of discarded pieces of other stories. Some had swapped parts with others. Who had made these stories? Who had left all these stories behind? Bardo hadn't clearly seen the stories before, although he had hints they were there. He had felt them when he swam and fragments of them unfamiliar to him appeared in his mind, or when he was knee deep fishing and his thoughts turned to unusual parts of them. But now he could see multitudes of them floating and shining just below the surface. I wonder, he thought, if I can harvest just one of these stories, or myself make up just one and leave it in the sea. And, he wondered, how will my story end up in the sea with these others? He smiled. The sea around desde Desdemona, he could see, was really a library. Maybe, he thought, I can have one of these stories.

CHAPTER 2

▼

Bardo shakes his head and talks to himself. Exquisite sensuality, he grumbles. The seven course commemorative fiftieth birthday love making didn't quite happen. How could it? he asks. Before I could get to my birthday, I got trashed. He struggles upright in the hammock facing the reef. His dense, forest like Nixonian stubble has begun to re-emerge on his chest. It looks like black flecks of pepper or small mouse turds. It ends at the plastic neck brace. You, he says, looking at his unshaven face in the mirror as his head shakes from left and right, are dangerous to yourself and to others. In his throat he can feel coarse knots that might in season ripen into crying. He tries to identify the particular lack of mindfulness that has resulted in this unwanted, unexpected consequence. Why, he asks himself for the twenty-eighth time, did I get myself hurt? Why, he asks himself, did I come so close to an untimely death? He hears footsteps on the catwalk and begins to execute a slow motion, corkscrew maneuver to stand up. He is stiff and all of him hurts, inside and out.

"What's the other guy look like?" It is Marley Jameson. He is wearing a faded tie dye tee shirt, his dreadlocks are pushing out from under a Yankees baseball cap, and he is carrying a laptop computer in a woven cloth backpack.

"Please don't make me laugh, it'll hurt."

"Did you get the brace at central casting? I don't remember James Bond or any of the great covert action heroes ever wearing one of those. My ancestor William lived to 90 without even a broken toe nail." He pauses. "And what did you do with all your hair? You joining up with Thich Nhat Hanh or something?"

Bardo shuffles stiffly across the porch toward him. "It's just a shameless solicitation for your sympathy. It's my fiftieth birthday present to myself." He points in the general direction of his neck and head.

Marley frowns and puts the laptop in the corner. "Well, Nijinski," he says, "What happened?" He leans on the railing. Bardo tries unsuccessfully to find a comfortable way to stand or lean or tilt. Marley wants to hear the full story; Bardo, he realizes from past experiences, will edit it to just the subtitles or chapter headings. He waits while Bardo lists and shifts like a cork on the tide.

"A car accident. The night before my birthday, it was raining. A car plowed into me. Kaboom. Crash cars. All fall down. All my fault."

"Fortunately, nobody was hurt too much. Except me, and my feelings. I could've gotten killed. And I got a ticket."

"It's a replication of my birth pattern," Bardo ventures with a grimace. "Or acting out my death wish, one."

Marley scoffs at this analysis. "Oh yeah?" he smirks, "A little of both birth and dying? You know, we could've beat you up and sung happy birthday to you at the same time before you left and saved you the accident. Why didn't you just ask us? Well, at least one of us has gratitude that there was nothing permanent in it. I guess you'll be all right."

Bardo's eyes are wet. He shrugs. "I don't know," he begins. "When I'm in the outside world, away from here working I usually believe in my competence, that I can function well in civilization, that I'm safe, that I have more time on the planet. So now I'm standing in desde Desdemona, where competence doesn't seem to matter a great deal, and I'm looking at vivid evidence of my own startling incompetence. I thought my second fifty would be lived with mastery. With skilfulness. Instead, look at me. I came really close to ending it. It is still scary to me." He shakes his head and frowns.

Marley looks at him. It's not a pretty picture. The neck brace is an odd, shiny, pearly color, and Bardo's listing slightly to the left. There is a taut, sweaty nervousness in his face and his eyes squint. Marley gently hugs Bardo to him.

"Stay with us, dude," Marley says into his ear. "Stay with us then." He gently pats him on the back.

✳   ✳   ✳   ✳

Bardo and Marley Jameson are both happy to be the occupational descendants of William Jameson. In the early 21st century posting desde Desdemona's reef with buoys and raising the black flag of plague won't keep people away. It might even attract film crews from the media or a reality television series. Instead, it has fallen to Bardo and Jameson to make desde Desdemona seem like fiction. It, Atlantis and Lemuria all don't appear on satellite weather maps or National Geographic maps, even if they are all on the world wide web and are all linked to each other. That's why there are no direct flights. The final flight has to be by sea plane. There are no telephone or other cables to the island. There is no cell phone service. There are no UN missions and no embassies and no American Express. The currency is traded only on the island. There are no passports. There is no attempt to halt or discover terrorists. The web sites, all run by the Ministry of Limited Tourism, are a contradictory, disparaging, intimidating tangle of fact and fiction. Mail arrives once a week, retrieved from a single post office box on a neighboring island. The travel channel has never visited. Books that mention the island are in the fiction section, where they huddle binding to binding with stories of walkabouts with the Aborigines and trips with Peruvian Shamans. These books are never found in the travel section. There is no Lonely Planet Guide to desde Desdemona. Desde Desdemona is not in geography classes, the UN, or FIFA, the world soccer organization. It does not participate with other countries in anything.

All of desde Desdemona's neighbors are simply delighted to claim that the island nation is nothing but a charming fantasy, a rare mythological, rather than geological formation. They perpetuate the stories that tell how the island migrates from place to place in the sea, appearing and disappearing with the tides, that it has a long history of rumors and legends, but really does not exist. It, they say, is just an allegory for themselves. It's like Santa Claus or the Tooth Fairy. Her neighbors all claim that they are the true desde Desdemona and attribute the name to various pirates, exiles, artists, and wanderers. With a mocking wink and a nod, the island is repeatedly claimed to be a mirage or a hallucination. But despite all of it, stories persist about the beauty of the female occupants of the island, that they are really the Sirens.

Occasionally someone claims to have been to desde Desdemona. These stories are immediately greeted in the neighboring countries with hoots or knowing scoffs and gestures about the head, as if they were tales of alien abduction or interspecies communication or telepathy or psychokinesis.

*   *   *   *

Building tree houses and catwalks was grueling physical work, but throughout Oscar's years of labor the sea nourished him. The water was calm, warm enough that he could sit or stand neck deep in it for hours, cool enough in the mid day heat to refresh, and full of fish to eat. He loved to sit in water up to his chest, talking with Milagros, while their children splashed and swam around them. He loved to float on his back, rocking gently, looking at the sky, feeling the warmth of the sun on his face and belly. It was amazing to him that he could float for more than an hour. Eventually, with practice, he became so relaxed in the sea, that he could close his eyes, focus on his breath, and fall asleep while floating.

Soon simultaneously floating and napping became one of Oscar's favorite activities; he loved to fall asleep and nap while floating, slowly rocking on the gentle swell, totally relaxing his arms and legs.

When he fell asleep in the water, he drifted slightly. Sometimes he drifted in to shore, sometimes toward open water. When he awoke, he was continually surprised that he had slept, and then, refreshed, he swam back to desde Desdemona, however far away that might then be. His longest nap, Oscar thought, took him 1,000 meters from the island.

Most remarkable to him about his naps was Oscar's dreaming. In his dreams the dolphins appeared and talked with him about their migratory life, telling him stories about the delights of cities in Atlantis and Lemuria, their difficult relationships and occasional conflicts with the mermaids, the family life of whale communities, and the cooperation and peace that flourishes in their pods. When Oscar awoke, he might be unsure whether he had been dreaming, but he could easily recall the vivid images the dolphins transmitted, and he discovered that these images were easily summoned into his waking consciousness. He savored these images, turning them over and over again in his mind while he worked, enjoying their sweetness and gentleness, turning them slowly like a glinting diamond in the sun. He found them precious.

Oscar should not have been surprised in the slightest when one of his floating naps was interrupted by a dolphin. But he was. The dolphin, whose name was Lisette, swam silently next to Oscar while he was asleep. Then she put her right flipper between his legs. Oscar, despite all his dreams about dolphins and his receiving images from them for so long, and despite his initial, unforgettable swim with one, did not understand that dolphins are perpetually at the brink of sexual arousal and that this sort of playful greeting was commonplace to them. He awoke with a colossal start, flinching so deeply that he inhaled water and began an earthquake-like tremor of coughing. At this, Lisette started whistling and grinning and laughing and squealing with delight at how effective her joke was. Oscar continued to sputter and flail and choke until she steadied him by embracing him, pulling his chest against her and holding him upright, face out of the water, with both flippers, until he finally relaxed and his breathing returned to its rhythm.

While Lisette cuddled Oscar, comforting messages appeared in his mind. "I'm sorry I scared you," Lisette was saying. "You're safe with me." The startle really upset Oscar. His mind was gasping for comprehension as his lungs had struggled for air. Lisette was soft, warm, gentle; he was being hugged by a dolphin who had a very strange sense of humor. Slowly, he began to relax. The spasm subsided. He recalled the surprising deliciousness of his first, quick dolphin embrace 8 years before, and thought to his utter surprise, "I hope there's more to this than last time."

At this the dolphin exploded in splashing laughter. "Just enjoy being with me now," Lisette was saying. Eventually, she released Oscar from her embrace, transported him to the edge of the beach, and swam off. In Oscar's mind an indelible message appeared, "Let's learn to play together; I will visit you again soon. Try not to inhale water when you are surprised."

As he walked up the beach, an enormous grin appeared on Oscar's face. Did that dolphin goose me? he wondered.

*   *   *   *

Milagros was eating a mango when Oscar arrived. "The most amazing thing," he said. He noticed how her sticky fingers glistened, and felt an ache in his chest at the beauty of her mouth and mocha colored throat. "I have to tell you right now."

Milagros laughed at his story. Her laugh sounded to Oscar a lot like Lisette's. "I'm not exactly surprised. When I have traveled on the sea to get the plants for our garden, I frequently dream of the dolphins when I sleep in the boat. And whenever I see them dancing across the sea, they send their messages and images to me, as I do to them. This was something I first learned from my grandmother, and she from her grandmother. They, like some of the other creatures, are trying to helping us. They help us even though humans have from time to time hunted and killed them. They are kind to us anyway. I like them very much; they are a good example. They are happy and peaceful and enjoy talking with us."

"Do you think I will see Lisette again?"

"I have never known dolphins to lie."

Milagros walked toward him, hugged him to her with her right arm, sliding her mango covered left hand down his belly and into his pants. "I have learned a great deal from the dolphins," she said into his ear. "And you see, I have also learned not to startle you."

*   *   *   *

The sea marooned Arjuna and Saraswati Chowdhary on desde Desdemona after six days at sea. Arjuna was horrified. The bottom of their boat was broken open by the reef, and the heavy suitcase full of money they had with them was almost lost. Their ultimate destination, Trinidad, had been meticulously and completely planned by Arjuna, and they were right on course except for one thing. They collided with an island that was not on their map. They ran aground on a reef that as far as the map makers were concerned, could not exist.

Arjuna was furious. "What kind of island is this, anyway?" he shouted at no one in particular, kicking the sand on the beach, stomping his foot. Tears of frustration jumped from his eyes. "The ocean is supposed to be hundreds of feet deep here!" he bellowed. "There is not supposed to be an island. No reef. Nothing but deep, deep ocean. I'm not off course. This is not Trinidad, damn it." His plan, which then seemed to be in serious jeopardy, was to take his money, put it in the bank in Trinidad, live like a very rich man, which he then was, have a lot of children with Saraswati, and ultimately to pursue his interest in spirituality with great mystic teachers he would find.

Saraswati considered telling him to stop acting like a baby. At least, she thought, they hadn't drowned. And they did find dry land. Maybe, she thought, he could even be thankful. And, she thought with faint pleasure as he raged on, now we are even again. The departure for this journey was shakey, and that was my fault, but the score has now been tied. This particular, quite eventful mistake belongs to him and to him alone, she thought with great satisfaction.

She had seen his tantrums in the face of the unexpected before; she decided to say nothing. She sat down on the beach and made small furrows in the sand with her fingers while her husband conducted a raging dialogue with himself about the unfairness and injustice of the present situation. Eventually, she thought, this storm will blow itself out.

Then Arjuna saw in a tree nearby a rope ladder and a tree house. He pointed, "We're not alone here!" The sudden discovery terminated his dramatic presentation. He ran across the beach toward the tree and grabbed the rope ladder. Looking up, he saw above a railing the smiling face of Oscar. "Bienvenidos," said Oscar in Spanish.

Arjuna exploded in a torrent of words at the face above him. He was speaking in English, a language Oscar did not know, and he was talking at a million miles an hour. Even if Oscar spoke English, he would have had trouble understanding Arjuna's accent and gattling gun delivery. Oscar watched. He wondered how Arjuna could say so much in a single breath. "Soon he will have to stop to breathe," Oscar thought, "Then I'll be able to talk with him." While Arjuna was reciting his litany of travails like a runaway freight, Oscar called to Milagros to bring the baby and see that someone had arrived, that their boat was wrecked and lying on its side and that they should probably take these people in before the return of the tide.

Before Arjuna was finished with the first dramatic verse of his paean on the just concluded heroic sea voyage, Saraswati arrived at the bottom of the rope ladder lugging a knapsack and dragging a suitcase across the rapidly disappearing beach. Her arrival stunned Arjuna into sullen silence. "What," he worried to himself, "will happen if these people we have discovered here try to take my money? What will stop them? What can I do to protect our money?"

Milagros's face appeared over the railing above. She looked down and saw a sullen, very thin, dark skinned, dark haired man in dirty clothing biting his lip, and a small woman with long, thick hair struggling with the couple's belongings. She handed the baby to Oscar, hurried down the ladder, and gestured that she wanted the two to come above, that the beach was rapidly disappearing. At that, Oscar, too, ran down the ladder, handed the baby back to Milagros, and stomped through three inches of incoming tide. He seized the boat, which had a gaping hole in its bottom and a matching one on its side, and tied it to a tree. Then, like Milagros, he gestured that the couple should immediately climb the ladder.

Later, as he sat in the tree house eating grilled fish, salad, and fried platanos, drinking rain water, and watching the setting sun send streaks of red across the sky, Arjuna realized that he was no longer on a journey. Ready or not, he had arrived. He was comfortable and safe and nobody knew or even seemed to care what was in his suitcase. Oscar and Milagros, he thought, were doing quite well, miraculously well in paradise. Maybe his plans needed to be slightly, beneficently revised.

Saraswati noticed that for the first time in weeks Arjuna seemed not to be so wary, that his eyes were not darting from place to place, that his face and brow had slightly relaxed. After eating, she walked with Milagros through the plants and she looked at the baby asleep in a tiny hammock strung between two papaya trees. The child was fast asleep on his back with its arms and legs spread wide open. His breathing was deep and rhythmic in his belly. Saraswati, who had seen many babies asleep and who thought often about having babies with Arjuna, was surprised that the boy was not in the fetal position. She had never seen any baby sleep like that before.

The boy, she later learned, had been born beneath the sea. Dolphin midwives had assisted Milagros and Oscar to birth him just off shore. He slept as he first appeared on the planet under the sea, arms and legs spread wide, thoroughly relaxed and filling his space with Atlantean grace.

CHAPTER 3

▼

It's Sunday. Bardo is exultant. As soon as the tide recedes, the soccer game on the beach will resume, as it does every Sunday at the first low tide, as it has for the past 50 years or so.

There was once a soccer league in desde Desdemona. It had 7 very evenly matched teams with names. Men and women played, and children 7 and up played. It used to be that being on a particular team was for a lifetime; any disparities between teams were erased by age and its buddies, slowness and death, the return of teenagers from prep schools and colleges, and tourists who were always invited to play. A team won a game if it created a blow out and was 3 or more goals ahead when the tide returned. Closer games were never ended, they just resumed when the field reappeared and stopped when exhaustion made breaks in the game too long or too frequent. When events in 1978 destroyed the league, "the game" as it is now called, took the league's place.

In 1978 Perico Azul and Playa de Luna, fueled by the return of college players, were the best teams in the league. Their game had lasted 7 sessions and was dead-locked at 1-1, despite the best efforts of the players. The league destroying incident arose as the tide lapped at the sidelines. On a Perico Azul corner kick, the goal keeper, John Coltrane Ramirez, tried to punch the ball out of the mouth of the goal. Instead of flying safely away, over the heads of the then swarming offense, the uncooperative ball hit the heal of the keeper's hand and slammed into the back of a Perico striker. At that precise moment, the striker's back was turned to the goal and his hand was against it as he tried to swat an insect that, having crawled up his back, was trying to drain his blood. Depending on which side of the dispute one wishes to enter, the ball hit the striker's back <u>or</u> his hand,

and rolled into the goal as stunned defending players unsuccessfully dove at or chased after it. The field immediately erupted in arguments in three languages. Perico players, thinking they had scored, rejoiced. Playa players yelled, insisting vociferously there had been a hand ball, and that, as a consequence, the goal could not and did not count. Melvin Gandhi, a Playa sweeper, could be seen jumping up and down in splenetic rage, screaming over the din in high pitched, accented English, "It is an outrage. I tell you. I tell you. In all of my entire life on this island I never have seen such an incorrect play." Meanwhile, the Perico players who were not red in the face arguing, danced in circles, chanting "Me gusta, Me gusta, Me gusta!"

In desde Desdemona there are no referees. The din immediately turned to complete silence and all the players turned to the striker whose back <u>or</u> whose hand had touched the ball. The idea, inculcated in all desde Desdemona players and practiced from infancy on, was that the player who was involved would directly and truthfully tell what had happened. This, it was supposed, would immediately and finally end all the arguments and permit the game to proceed. There would be no "Hand Of God" goal in desde Desdemona. There just couldn't be, it was thought.

The striker then explained how he had turned, how he was trying to remove the bug. And then to the utter astonishment of everyone, he said, "I'm just not sure."

Spurred by this egregious lack of mindfulness all the arguments resumed with renewed fury.

Only the returning tide and the flooding of the field disbursed the arguing players. Out of desde Desdemona's national sense of pride in its national attribute, compassion, the particular striker's name has become a secret. His name is never mentioned in connection with the incident although he still resides on the island and the older players remember his name and his legendary offense.

Word of the incident and what by then was either the striker's public confession of unconsciousness or, what was worse, an outright falsehood, spread through the island. It was impossible, even for those on the North Coast, who were renunciates living without possessions in the ashram, not to have an argumentative position or a judgmental opinion on the event and the entirely too human, deficient state of desde Desdemona's mass consciousness. The event vaporized their long sought after equanimity.

And all those on the island who unlike the renunciates, never even considered renouncing gossip or not speaking their judgments of other people, were absolutely thrilled to incite arguments and delighted to spread their critical opinions to anyone who would listen. By evening, it was clear that players would have to leave all the other teams in the league, and that, depending on which side of the dispute they believed in, join either Playa or Perico. It was a matter of pride and societal importance. The game had to be ended with the correct result, whatever that might have been, and the partisans each thought they could help produce the blow out that would end the game, producing justice and tranquility, and balancing karma in one fell shot on goal.

That was in 1978. The game Bardo was about to resume was now 196 to 195, with Playa on top. And Bardo, his chest and back hair regrown, like the other 50 and 60 year olds in the game, would begin with good intentions, but as air became scarce and sweat plentiful, his best defense would be not so surreptitiously hanging on his opponent's jersey like a cement block anchor. This would bring encouragement from John Coltrane Ramirez, who was still in goal, and who with the slowed reflexes of a 60 year-old needed all the help his aging defense could muster.

*   *   *   *

Children in desde Desdemona have their own game. It is like telephone or Roshomon. From 7 to 14 children sit in a circle. One person whispers something to her neighbor, who then passes it on. But in desde Desdemona each player intentionally changes what was whispered in the slightest fashion before passing it on. The goal, collectively realized, is to have the last person correctly repeat the initial phrase. Unlike telephone or Roshomon, which are based on the importance of repeating with accuracy, the game in desde Desdemona celebrates as important the interdependent causes of all events. The game is called, "Grapefruits from the cobbler."

The name comes from an adage frequently told to island youngsters by their parents. In the story, a man who wants a grapefruit goes to various merchants looking for the fruit. None of them has a grapefruit because they sell hardware, or goats, or birds, or eggs, or shoes. Parents in desde Desdemona repeatedly try to explain to their children not to ask for various kinds of grapefruits from someone who is selling something else. If you want grapefruits, they say, you must go to the grapefruit seller.

*   *   *   *

Arjuna was not surprised to discover that he actually liked being in desde Desdemona. Life on the island was relatively easy. He had no real use for his money and he had nothing to worry about. He built a home and he worked with Oscar on the tasks of planting fruit, growing herbs and catching fish. The island, he thought, was daily making Saraswati even more beautiful, even more attractive to him. And it seemed to him that the same must be happening to him: Saraswati was always at his side, always touching his hand or arm, always putting her arm around him, wanting, as he did, to make love morning and night. What else, he thought, could he possibly desire? But there was, when he asked this question, something missing. How, he asked himself, was he going to receive on desde Desdemona the spiritual instruction that was inextricably intertwined in his desire to make his initial voyage? The spiritual instruction he was seeking when he left home? Maybe they should leave. Maybe they should fix the boat or get a new one and continue their journey. How else could he accomplish his original goal?

When he confided this thought to Saraswati, she laughed. "Have you asked for a teacher or are you just going to dream about it?" she asked. Then, referring to an old version of Grapefruits from Cobblers, she chuckled, "And it's a shame there's no donkey merchant here."

Arjuna's dreams had been quite vivid and, as far as he was concerned, they were speaking about this very issue. In one recurring dream, the king of sea serpents, Dhumavarna, came up to him on the beach at low tide. "Arjuna," the king hissed like a steam engine, "My five beautiful mermaid daughters want to meet you, they want you to marry them and father their children. Come into the water and let me carry you away to them." Arjuna was thrilled that someone so obviously important as a Naga King should emerge in his dreams, but he was also frightened by the enormity of the sea serpent king, and afraid that this request might be a serpentine artifice to devour him. On the other hand, simultaneous marriage to the five, slippery, beautiful mermaid daughters certainly kindled his lust. He could deeply and profoundly enjoy fathering their children. So he responded, "I am most complimented, your Majesty. But I cannot leave desde Desdemona until the true teacher arrives here. Then I will be ready seriously to consider your offer." The utterance of the cryptic answer in the direction of His Hissing Majesty woke Arjuna. Rolling over toward Saraswati in the hammock, he spoke in her jasmine scented ear, "Dhumavarna's trying to trick me into leaving, trying to entice me, but I want to find the guru first." Then he fell back asleep.

In Arjuna's other dream he encountered the ascetic named "Matanga," who was standing on one foot chanting mantras. Matanga, legend had it, was the off-spring of a secret liaison between a married Brahmin woman and a low caste man. Raised as a Brahmin, one day Matanga beat a donkey with a stick. The donkey responded, "This is just what I expect from one of lowly birth." Matanga was shocked at this horrifying allegation about his caste, and asked the donkey just what she meant by this horrendous slander. Upon hearing the explanation, Matanga immediately became a renunciate, standing on one toe for a hundred years, until Indra taught him to fly.

No words passed between Arjuna and Matanga. Instead, Arjuna watched for a long time while Matanga miraculously stood in the one toe tree pose and chanted. The dream awoke him with the thought that single mindedness and determination were required of him if he were to prevail. "I have to remain true to it," he thought on waking. "I have to have find the teacher. I have to finish the planned ocean journey."

While he and Oscar were hauling three heavy mango trees from the dugout and up the walkway, Arjuna, after yet another evening double feature of serpents and balancing ascetics, decided he should explain to Oscar, his companion, his long held desire for a spiritual teacher. This, Arjuna thought optimistically, might be difficult. Oscar speaks a few words of English; I know only a few words of Spanish. I will act it out for him.

But Arjuna's impatience stalked his every charade. Almost immediately, he was jumping up and down, kicking the sand, shouting, turning red, dancing concentric circles of the frustration. Saraswati and Milagros, who heard the commotion, came running. "Husband!" Saraswati shouted, "Are you hurt?"

"How do I show him that I love it here, but that I need to find a spiritual master to teach me?" Arjuna screeched, the words like hurricane raindrops splattering on a tin roof. "I can't act it out. I can't speak his language."

At this Saraswati started to whoop. Turning to Oscar and Milagros, Saraswati explained in perfect, but slow Spanish, "My husband needs a teacher. He wants to become enlightened."

Oscar's mouth fell open. "What's that got to do with elephants? I thought he wanted it to rain elephants here. Or that planets and meteors were about to fall on this island."

"Husband, why were you telling him about Ganesha if you just wanted a teacher to come here?" Ganesha is the god with the head of an elephant, the first god one prays to for the granting of wishes and the removal of obstacles.

Arjuna started to stammer and he teetered on the brink of again jumping up and down, but Saraswati and Milagros instead took him by the hands and led him gently to the tree house. "Be calm," soothed Saraswati. "It'll be all right."

"We'll show you how to get the teacher," Milagros said in perfect, but halting English.

$$*\qquad*\qquad*\qquad*$$

Milagros and Saraswati had discovered to their mutual delight that they were both masters of manifestation, who could make something appear from seeming nothing. Instead of the lead alchemists needed to make gold, Milagros and Saraswati needed only pure, focused intention to materialize something, even matter, from nothing. It was their concerted activities that led to the ship wreck.

Milagros evidently was not exaggerating when she told Arjuna that she and Saraswati would shortly produce a spiritual master for him on desde Desdemona. She neglected, however, to explain that they would produce not only the master but some disciples as well and that they would produce this entire ashram within six weeks.

On a perfect morning, shortly after sunrise, Arjuna awoke to what he thought was the sound of a harmonium and the chanting of disciples. Who could be chanting "Om Nama Shivaya" in this ocean?" he asked. Is this now the Indian Ocean? The Andaman Islands? Sri Lanka? Has desde Desdemona migrated that far from the Caribbean? Looking out to sea, he saw a schooner that was entirely too close to the reef with no one at the helm. The red trident of Shiva was affixed to the top of the mast. He woke Saraswati. As they watched and listened, the ship for no apparent reason climbed onto the reef and ripped in two while the sounds of the harmonium and chanting to honor Shiva filled the air. The six passengers fell into the water shouting with surprise and swam to the beach.

"And so you see what happens when mindfulness is absent?" said the little, round man in the drenched, pale yellow robe, giggling.

"How can you laugh at a time like this?" asked a younger man, who like the first, was in a drenched robe and had a shaved head, but who, unlike the first, was indignant.

The little, round man responded to this with peals of squealing laughter. The laughter immediately infected two other people, one a man and one a woman, also wearing soaked robes, and they too began to giggle and then laugh uncontrollably. Tears flowed from the little round man's eyes as he laughed.

"This is definitely what happens when mindfulness is absent," the little round man said again, roaring with laughter.

Oscar and Arjuna dragged the largest pieces of the vessel to the beach and tied them up, much to the relief of the sailor and his wife, the only two people not wearing robes, who were busy convincing themselves that the ship could be easily refloated and that they were not stranded on a tropical island and that they would soon be able to return to the predictability of their distant home, that only a few repairs would be needed.

Milagros and Saraswati, meanwhile, welcomed the teacher and his disciples to desde Desdemona. The teacher, referred to by his students simply as "Sri Swamiji", was crammed full of parables, stories, homilies, synopses of holy books, knowledge of the teaching of the great arhats and bodhisattvas, and meditations, all seasoned with gales of laughter and delight.

Sri Swamiji put his palms together and bowing to Milagros and Saraswati, said, "Namaste! Such a powerful invitation! Such a strong call!" At this he started again to howl with laughter, his entire body shaking, his eyes tearing. "So much more powerful than putting a note in a bottle!" The squealing laughter was like a flock of wheezing geese. "Where is that one, the badmash, who put you up to this?" he said. Then eying Arjuna from head to toe as if measuring him for a suit, Swamiji nodded, "Oh, we can do what you want, what you called me here for. It is for certain. We can do exactly what you want!" Then Swamiji tilted his head back and resumed his laughing.

CHAPTER 4

▼

"You always leave out the important parts of the story," Ona tells Bardo. They are lying in a hammock, waiting for the afternoon return of the children from school, watching the pelicans circle the reef. "If many interconnected events caused something to happen, you would leave out most of the causes and you'd probably leave out most of the result, too."

It was true. Bardo's best form of expression was e-mail, a quick sentence or two, no introduction, no denouement, just blurting it out. If he told an anecdote, by the end of the first sentence his mind was sending alarm signals that he was probably talking too much. Most of his ideas, he thought, could be expressed in 4 sentences, and his feelings, once he found out what they were, in two. He simply couldn't stand to retell events by reciting chronologically exactly what people said and what they did. He always edited and paraphrased, and he often omitted the details of what people actually said and did because he had already abstracted them and forgotten these details.

But he loved the richness of Ona's expression, the unedited, untrammeled, free flowing cascade of the events of the day, analyses surfacing like a pod of dolphins in the midst of a mirror like sea of narration, the digressions like waves crashing on the beach, the cul de sacs, the rolling, foaming alternation of theme and variations, the continuous eruptions of insights, analyses, comparisons, asides tumbling round and round and finally ebbing slowly to a close. He loved to listen to her narrate the events of her day. In his mind it was the music of the sea or revelation of one of the beautiful, rich, pearl like stories floating just off shore in the sea. He wondered whether she had any idea at all how much he enjoyed how she told her stories. But sometimes, in exasperation, he would interrupt or beg her to get to the point, and at those times, his impatience seemed oddly out of place in desde Desdemona, unnecessary, and slightly cruel, incongruous like the sharp scrub cactus clutching the rocks on the leeward side of the island.

She is, of course, entirely right; he should not have interrupted what she was saying. There was no reason for his haste, and his impatience, his distraction was, as usual, merely a measure of his preoccupation with his other concerns. He waits to see whether she will resume her story. He can see the pelicans diving near the reef, and he can hear the children's running footsteps on the walkways. He notices, while he waits for her to resume her tale, that his breath is now deeper and slower and that the breeze again smells slightly of eucalyptus.

The children, Ona resumes, had been alarmed that morning by stories and news video of the activity of a nearby volcano and the likely evacuation of endangered islanders from their homes to other islands. Sometimes she wishes the children could be more fully isolated from the television images that reach the island by satellite. It cannot be a good thing for a seven year old to dwell on the frequent violence in the broadcasts. She is happy that her children do not watch much television.

The videos showed billowing, noxious smoke towering into the sky, blocking the light of the sun, burning cottages, and there were orange, smoking rivulets of molten lava. There was talk that the entire population of the island would have to be evacuated. The kids understood that they were safe in desde Desdemona, but they wanted to know if we were going to invite any of the displaced people to find refuge here. She told them that it was something we would all discuss immediately. Jeremy, Ona said, thought it was particularly important to help these people as swiftly as we can. Eleven year olds season helping others and concerns about what's fair with outright defiance of authority. He asked, "If the volcano were in desde Desdemona, would our neighbors take us all in?" Ona said she thought they would; he didn't seem at all convinced. He said he thought that the neighbors of desde Desdemona think we are all weird and that they probably would make us move to the United States. He didn't seem to like the idea of that. Ona wondered if the neighbors thought they were weird. She could understand why they might think that.

*   *   *   *

Sri Swamiji was more than Arjuna bargained for. Arjuna thought his spiritual quest was serious business, that it might require asceticism, acute deprivation, or mysterious, painful, secret and arcane practices, but Swamiji would have none of this. Before he met Swamiji, Arjuna imagined that in his pursuit of spiritual enlightenment he would have to wake up at 4 am, stand in chest deep freezing water, and chant in dead Asian languages for hours. Despite Swamiji's telling him repeatedly that the process of reaching enlightenment had to be a pleasurable act, an act of love, an embracing of the divine, Arjuna would not, could not accept painlessness, let alone bliss and delight. Whenever Arjuna relapsed in stoicism or fanaticism, put on his serious mien and raised complicated questions about the true self, dualism, non-dualism, emptiness, enlightenment, and the like Swamiji began to laugh out loud. "Oh what questions!" Swamiji snickered. "Why are you asking me these questions, do you think I know the answers to them?"

"Well, actually," Arjuna responded, "Don't you?"

"Of course not, you silly man!" Swamiji exploded in laughter. "I only answer practical questions. You know that by now!" Usually the outburst infected the other disciples and they too would be convulsed.

"I told you many times," Swamiji said, "Just notice and appreciate the perfection in everything and feel your gratitude. When you have learned to do this, I will notice it and I will give you the next step. Meanwhile, eat nothing but watermelon."

"Why watermelon?" Swamiji anticipated. "Because it will help to develop your sense of humor." He found this remark hysterical and was again convulsed with a torrent of laughter which his disciples shared.

Arjuna dutifully wandered off in search of watermelon. "Is that why he laughs like that?" he wondered. None of the other disciples was eating only watermelon. This must be something he needed, a special prescription for his personal enlightenment. He looked out on the sea and saw Oscar asleep, floating on his back with Lisette pushing him toward the beach.

✳   ✳   ✳   ✳

After a particularly delicious comida tipica, the blowing of a conch announced the meeting. Separate meetings were held in each of the parts of desde Desdemona. Most of the tourists, although invited to watch the meetings, chose instead to sit in a hot tub on the deck, watch the half moon rise over the sea, and discuss with bountiful glasses of Chardonnay whether the volcanic ash was making the moon seem particularly yellow. The tourists, most of whom seemed to be from New York City, incorrectly conceived of the meeting as if it would resemble those held by boards of New York City cooperative apartment houses. They incorrectly thought to their dread that the meeting would interminably mix unfathomably boring subject matter with inexplicably hostile interactions, tantrums and threats. Hardly the recreation to be pursued in desde Desdemona, they surmised. Hardly conducive to relaxation.

Formal community meetings in desde Desdemona are convened very infrequently, and only when there is an immediate need for a community-wide decision. The meetings follow a format originally introduced by Saraswati and Milagros, designed to make the meeting a pleasure for all who attend.

Everyone present forms a tight circle, by crossing arms in front of themselves, and joining hands, left hand up, right hand down. There is silence. Everyone silently asks in an individual way for a wise resolution to the issue that will bring the most joy and peace. Then the oldest person present invites the sound of "om" and the group joins in. Whoever wishes to may then speak. The talk continues until there is unanimity. When consensus is reached, each person acknowledges agreement by saying, "Let it be." The youngest person present then invites the sound of "om" and the group joins in. The meeting is concluded.

The meeting immediately decided that some of the refugees should be invited to come to desde Desdemona. The harder questions involved how many people should be invited and how the people would be selected. These issues were immediately resolved. John Coltrane Ramirez said that he wanted to be sure that two of the people who came, one for each team, could run backwards faster than Bardo, who, regrettably was getting slow and tearing a lot of shirts now that he had reached 50. The mention of his age brought out ooohs from the crowd. One of the renunciates immediately chimed in that anybody could run faster backwards than Bardo, provoking both laughter and simultaneously a sharp look of disapproval from Swamiji. Why, said Jeremy, don't we just put out an invitation for up to 3 families and see who shows up, isn't that historically how desde Desdemona grew? This brought nodding of heads and an end of the meeting. The "om" was proudly invoked by 7 year old Rosa, who arrived at the meeting early, hoping that no one younger than she would arrive, and who with constantly increasing excitement determined that only people older than she were in attendance.

∗   ∗   ∗   ∗

The music is blaring from Bardo and Ona's house. It is salsa and its choro spins over and over and over, "Todo mi Corazo-o-o-on." Marley Jameson feels it vibrating the floor as he reaches the top of the ladder. He hopes he's not going to interrupt a private, intimate though frenetic moment between man and woman, and thinks about coming back later, but when he peeps cautiously over the top rung, he sees Bardo alone, wearing soccer shorts, dancing in circles with a huge 15 kilo watermelon, grinning.

"Oh man, I didn't know you were a devotee of Swamiji," he says, pulling himself into the tree house. "I thought you were Tibetan Buddhist or something like that. You're acting like old Arjuna. Next thing you know you'll be gossiping like his disciples and arguing with the soccer referees."

"You never tried this, Marley? It is simply incredible."

"I don't merengue with melons, if that's what you mean. I prefer a partner who is larger, different curves, and more human."

"I've been eating mostly watermelon for months."

Marley is speechless. He is going to say that Bardo's been looking a little thin, but to Marley's surprise, Bardo cuts him off and starts a speed-of-light, staccato rant about watermelons. He's gesturing wildly about being in the cucumber family, opening the second chakra, fostering sexuality and creativity, how you tell ripeness from the "thunk" sound, about kinds of seeds and kinds of melons and where they grow and how. Soon, though, he remembers himself and suddenly slams on the brakes. He shrugs. "I guess we need to go make an invitation to some refugees without bringing the entire world back to desde Desdemona."

Marley nods. The melon, he thinks, seems to be loosening Bardo's tongue, allowing his built-in editor to go on vacation, and that is a good development.

They high 5 and head for the sea plane. "Bardo," Marley says, "Let's make a side trip too and get some new reading material, ok? I need to find some fiction that's both humorous and sophisticated. It should have some spiritual material in it, and be somewhat inspiring, too."

"That's going to be a tall order, Marley. That's not the usual mix. Sure you wouldn't rather just read sexy and violent. There seems to be quite a lot of that." Watermelon or not, Bardo stifles a rant about global capitalism's effects on the variety and quality of available books.

As they begin their evasive flight from desde Desdemona, they hear on the radio that the volcanic eruption will require the evacuation of the entire island of St. Sebastian and that United Nations members are sending a flotilla of ships to the stricken island.

✳   ✳   ✳   ✳

Saraswati was not initially thrilled with Swamiji's advice for Arjuna. She realized that he would, of course, make of the prescribed watermelon eating an act of remarkable spiritual significance and that he would eat watermelon and nothing else exclusively and undeviatingly either until Swamiji gave him a reprieve or he starved himself into a coma. This could become, she feared, a tiresome act of martyrdom and the extensive harvesting of complaints.

The first three days of eating watermelon, Arjuna was morose and grumpy. He complained. But on the fourth day, Saraswati saw him jumping up and down, up and down, up and down on a plank on the lowest walkway, grinning and breathless. He jumped up and down for about fifteen minutes, absorbed and childlike. And on the sixth day, she noticed that he seemed remarkably much calmer. Only after ten days did Saraswati ask Arjuna how his eating watermelon exclusively was for him. He laughed. "I'm not crazy," he said grinning. "I've eaten some other things. I eat *mostly* watermelon. I feel pretty clear." He smiled. "Swamiji knows me pretty well. He knows the path. He is a good map maker. I think something is happening."

Saraswati could feel her passion for Arjuna rising in a blush. "Come home with me now," she whispered to him, taking his hand placing her arm around his waist. His hand was sticky and smelled of watermelon. There was a dried watermelon seed stuck to his pants.

CHAPTER 5

▼

Marley is frustrated. He's read all the soccer magazines in English, Spanish and German and most of the newspapers in the San Juan airport, and is thinking about starting to drink pina coladas to make the time pass. He can't find any books that he might like. He has had a waiting room nap, and his neck now aches. He and Bardo have been waiting at the gate for three hours. It has gone far beyond the jokes about BWIA meaning "But Will It Arrive." The UN flotilla, it seems, is responsible for grounding most flights. The gate area is filled with the two extremes of Caribbean travel: rich tourists, with fluorescent pallor when arriving and tanned or sunburnt when leaving, and the poor of color, leaving and coming home, carrying boxes taped shut with duct tape, crates, and battered suitcases. The tourists are vibrating with apparent anger at the humanitarian delay that has been imposed. The locals are implacably resigned to the wait and to show grace no matter what.

"I guess we're not supposed to get there too early," Bardo says. "I wonder what we're waiting for."

"I bet it means nothing. It's got nothing to do with us. Want to drink some rum? They have no Havana Club here, but we can make do."

"I like it until it gives me a headache. There's a reason we have to wait here."

"But you don't know what it is. So right now it doesn't matter." Marley frowns.

He looks at the clock and for the 47th time at the counter. The agent, who although exhausted from the questions and complaints of would be passengers is intent on appearing professional and acting like nothing is wrong, is stamping a ticket. Marley's eye is drawn to the richly cocoa colored arm of the passenger and to her back and to her hips and to her deep mahogany hair. She is short and thin and curvy. He finds her attractive, very attractive, extremely attractive. He finds that he is enjoying looking at her. He notices that he does not mind the delay nearly as much right now. He wonders if she will be assigned the seat next to him on the plane. That would be seat 13-C. Usually, he thinks, he is seated next to people he can't even talk to. Or next to people whose behinds are too ample for the seat and whose arms are like slabs of beef. He notices that she is carrying a laptop and a straw basket that is filled with small, yellow mangoes, and he can find no evidence that she is traveling with anyone else. He hopes that she will sit next to him and find him interesting. He thinks he finds her interesting.

Bardo is grinning. "I told you. I told you," he says. Marley is wondering if he has made any sounds or did anything else that may have tipped Bardo off. Bardo is obviously enjoying this. It is not every day that he gets to play the know-it-all.

"How do you know whether this is anything more than fantasy?" Marley asks the Omniscient One.

Bardo laughs out loud. He can see that her ticket envelope has the numbers 13-C on it in black magic marker. "Trust me on this one, ok dude?"

∗   ∗   ∗   ∗

It's 4 am and Arjuna is pacing in the tree house. He has been awakened by a frightening dream he cannot now recall. He notices that he is covered with sweat and that his heart is still pounding and his breath is quick and shallow. He tries to focus on deepening his breath, to calm his heart, to relax the tension throughout his body. He thinks about waking Saraswati. He thinks about waking Swamiji. No, he thinks, it's just a dream. I need to remember the dream. He closes his eyes and he thinks back into the dream. His breath catches in the midst of his inhale. I've already forgotten, he gasps. It's gone. No, he thinks, there it is. I'm remembering.

It is invulnerable Ravana. The ruler of the evil demons. He has assumed the shape not of the fearsome toothy being with 10 heads and 20 arms, but of a huge tower of smoke, of putrid, volcanic smoke. He is blocking the light of the sun and moon, and, having enveloped a small island, is pulling it up by its roots from the floor of the sea. He snarls and growls. He is shaking the island left and right, yanking it apart. Parts of it break open, leaving deep pits and lakes of molten lava. Houses crumble. They burst into flame and fall into the sea. People struggle to breathe. The smoke fills their eyes and mouths and they begin to burn. The animals on the island fall into the sea or the lava. A bright yellow bird, flying close to the sea, wheels around the cloud of smoke, and snatches from the sea five people, adults and children. She places them on her back, and flies off. The people hold on to the bird's back and to each other. They are amazed that of all the people on the island they should be fortuitously rescued by a bird.

"Who are the people?" Swamiji is asking. "Do you know?"

"That's where it ends, that's all I can remember."

"Continue to eat nothing but watermelon." Swamiji starts to giggle. The giggle grows into howls of red faced laughter. "And be sure to drink at least a gallon of water every day. Everything is becoming clear. Think about how you and the five are the same person."

Three of the disciples who hear this exchange think it appropriate to approach Arjuna later that day on the beach to say what a deep and important communication he has received from Swamiji. Arjuna, however, is incredulous. He doesn't know that anything out of the ordinary has occurred.

"What was deep?" he asks, between casts of his fishing net.

"Swamiji said to you it is becoming clear. That's a very important transmission. It is quite special."

"It might be clear to him, but it's not clear to me. Do you get to eat whatever you want?"

"Swamiji knows when things are getting clearer and he told you they were. That's very good indeed."

Arjuna shrugs. His net is flapping in the surf with a medium sized black snapper. Oscar and Milagros, he thinks, love to turn this kind of fish into ceviche. I will give it to them. I wish I could eat it. It's not a watermelon. I never catch watermelon.

"We're allowed to eat fish," one of the disciples says magnanimously.

At this Arjuna laughs out loud. "I'll teach you how to catch them, if you'd like." The disciples look at each other. They begin a rapid fire communication that is apparently an exegesis and analysis of a proverb that you can feed someone for a day if you give him a fish, but you can feed a village if you teach him to fish.

"We don't want to appear impatient, but can you show us this immediately, right now?" they laugh. Their robes are already wet at the bottom, from standing in the water with Arjuna, and they are imagining how many thousands of fish they can bring to the ashram, and how delighted the other disciples will be that they have had this opportunity.

"The key to catching fish," Arjuna says with conviction, "is availability. And not gossiping. Gossip drives the fish away. Gossip," he says, "Is talking about people who are not present." Both disciples nod; both wonder if they have some-how been admonished.

*   *   *   *

Ceviche de la Desdemona

The key is cutting the fish or shellfish or scallops into very small pieces. Not too small to eat with a fork. Not too large, either, so that the lime/lemon will pene-trate the entire piece. The lime/lemon cooks the fish.

1 1/2 lbs fish or scallops or shell fish cut in small pieces
1 cup lime juice
1/2 cup lemon juice
1/2 tsp minced jalapeno pepper or dried hot chili pepper
2 large cloves or more of garlic chopped
1 medium sized red onion chopped
1 tbsp or more of fresh cilantro chopped
1/2 tbsp cumin
1/2 tsp sea salt
Mix together and cool for 3 hours. Eat.

*   *   *   *

Originally, Marley conceived of the flight from San Juan to Barbados in his usual terms, part of an evasive maneuver required to preserve the peace and tran-quility of desde Desdemona from people who were uninvited interlopers. But he is unsettled by the events at the airport, the seating of a beautiful television news reporter next to him on the flight, and Bardo's repeated sidelong glances to see what he is up to with her.

"You can't fly into San Sebastian any more," she is saying. "So I'm going to Barbados to meet the refugees when they arrive there. It's a pretty big story. Why are you going?"

"We're going to pick some people up," Marley responds. He doesn't like being evasive with her. He is pretty sure that it undermines the possibility of a relationship with her if he dissembles at all, especially at the start, but he also knows he mustn't talk with her about desde Desdemona. He doesn't question for an instant his assumption that he will have a relationship with her.

"Are you with a relief agency?" she asks.

Marley nods, pointing at Bardo, "We're just going to Barbados, then we're leaving." The non sequitur bothers him. His evasiveness, something he's used to, is suddenly bothering him. "I bet your work is exciting."

It turns out that Mari Estrella has been covering Caribbean news for three or four years, and that she has heard from the beginning stories of an island that comes and goes, emerges and submerges, where the women are radiant as the Sirens, and where lucky tourists, who are invited, really relax. There are, she has heard, secret invitations to various people to visit the island, but she was never been able to confirm any of these stories. Has he ever heard about this?

Marley and Bardo have heard quite a lot about it, as it turns out. And Bardo is particularly interested in what she has heard about it. "But if you have to agree to keep it a secret if you've been there," Marley hypothesizes, "Nobody who talks about it is really reliable. And anyway," he says, "you're in the news media, so probably nobody there would believe that you would keep it a secret."

At this she frowns. "I keep my sources a secret and I protect them. I'd keep that island a secret, too, if I promised I would." He weighs this. He thinks it's hopeful. That she is committed to idealism, to integrity makes her even more infinitely desirable, more jewel like to him.

Marley can feel in his chest and stomach that he wants to invite her home to desde Desdemona and make passionate love to her. He wonders whether he is making up fantasies. The pilot is saying to put on seat belts and lift tray tables for the landing in Barbados. He is going to lose her when she leaves seat 13-C, he thinks. The situation is changing rapidly, he thinks. The opportunity, if that's what this is, may be vanishing. The stewards are in the aisle inspecting the seats and spraying insecticide in the aisle of the plane. "I hope this doesn't sound crazy, but I want to get to know you." The plane is vibrating, and then bumping down the runway.

She hands him a business card, looks straight into his eyes, puts her hand on top of his, and says, "I'd like that. And I promise to keep the secret." Then she kisses him swiftly on the cheek, fishes her laptop out from under the seat, walks down the aisle, the basket of mangoes swinging musically, and into the bright Barbados sunlight. The air smells slightly of sulphur. She is really beautiful.

"Oh man," Bardo is saying. "I told you there was a reason." They get off the plane, enter the terminal and buy two coconut ice cream cones. On a television screen, hanging above the ice cream concession, is the video of the plume of smoke and film of boats gliding across a shining sea. The voice is saying that the first of the boats will be arriving in Barbados shortly and that there will be exclusive coverage from the Caribe network reporter on the scene.

Hailing a cab, Marley and Bardo head for downtown Bridgetown and the embassy where arrangements for picking up the refugees will be completed.

*   *   *   *

Oscar is floating and sleeping in the sea. Lisette frolics nearby. Every so often she gives Oscar a gentle push toward desde Desdemona and samples his dream. Oscar is dreaming, as he often does, of the dense, triple canopy jungles of Guyana. He is involved with an enormous python gliding around in the limbs of a kapok tree. He is dreaming the hum of the insects and the cries of howler monkeys. He is dreaming a tall acacia tree and its stream of ants. Lisette is amazed at these images; she is stunned by how lush they are, the depth of the greens and how full of warm, wet oxygen they are. She loves the smell of the wet, living earth. To her, they are precious emeralds, and she carries them as a bejewelled adornment of her heart. They are Oscar's most valuable gift to her. When she is swimming with the pod, and the others ask to see them, she shows the other dolphins these treasures, and they too admire them.

The oldest dolphins tell the youngest that long ago, they lived on land, land that was as green and alive as Oscar's dreams, but that they eventually decided as a group to enter the sea and live there and not to return to land. The youngest dolphins always ask why this choice was made. The oldest always smile and say that even then they were able to see the future and that it was an extremely wise choice.

CHAPTER 6

▼

Bardo and Marley are alone in the ambassador's office. The ceiling fans are hardly moving, and shutters let in bands of bright light that make hash marks across the rug. There are satin flags standing in the corner. The "small favor" that the ambassador and foreign ministers from four Caribbean countries have "requested" has enraged Bardo while it intrigues Marley.

"They are absolutely threatening us," Bardo seethes. He's so angry he can't sit down. He paces. His fists are rolled up tight. "If we don't take him, they'll probably put on a commercial about desde Desdemona in the middle of the Super Bowl, or bring a cruise ship of travel writers, or put us back on the satellite maps. I don't see how we can say no. They think they control everything, and as far as I can tell, they probably do." Bardo stifles a polemic on globalization and imperialism.

Marley is pacing, too. "Us saying no is not the problem. We can't do that. Him saying yes is the real problem."

At that, there is a knock on the door, and a man in olive drab jungle fatigues enters. He has a close cropped beard and carries a red beret in his hand. He is muscular, short, and his eyes are afire. He looks just as he has on television, when he's been denouncing the government of San Sebastian and demonizing US interventionism, only thinner, more charming, more energetic, more bronze.

"They are making you take me?" he asks, extending his hand to Bardo and then Marley, and smiling. He doesn't need to say his name. They all know it. "Everybody else has a reason why they can't. Even Fidel. I thought Fidel would help me. I was wrong. I spend all this time turning the San Sebastian Liberation Front into a true Marxist party of opposition, exposing the contradictions of the ruling class, working for the dictatorship of the proletariat…" At this he cuts himself off. "Pardon my rhetoric, but those pig assholes are trying to send me and my family to someplace where it often snows, where you can regularly see the aurora borealis. Can you imagine the arrogance of that?"

"Canada?" asks Marley, who is about to sing the Canadian national anthem, extol the beauties of Labatt beer and Saturday hockey night, and praise Canada for its courage while the US was destroying Viet Nam to save it. Marley notices that no matter what, he does not want Acero to become angrier.

"Finland," he says. "They want to send me someplace that's 5000 kilometers to the nearest papaya. Where they drink Vodka." The "V" in vodka is said with an explosion as if it were a "B". "Where it snows 9 months of the year and there's no sun for 4. Western Canada would be ok. That's what they threaten me with. What are they threatening you with?"

Bardo and Marley both notice all of a sudden that they like Manuel Acero, leader of the San Sebastian Liberation Front. And they understand why the others are so afraid of him and would like to make him disappear from public view. He is vibrant and extremely powerful. They enjoy looking at him and the bright twinkle in his eyes. Bardo thinks it would be fun to play soccer with him. Maybe he's a midfielder. Bardo is unsure.

"Have you heard of desde Desdemona?" Bardo asks.

"Of course," he replies. "Fidel was invited there, right? And you made him promise not to tell anybody. That's very funny. You ask a guy who routinely talks extemporaneously to a crowd for 12 hours straight without any specific agenda, who digresses without worrying about whether he can ever get back to his main theme, to keep a secret. Fidel loves gossip. Anyway, he told me all about it, but I thought it was a bunch of bull and that he was pulling my leg. He claimed it relaxed him and that nobody there bothered him or interrupted his relaxation or questioned him about anything."

Bardo remembers Fidel's visits. How he dressed in yellow Bermuda shorts and grubby t-shirts, his Churchill cigar hanging from his hand and how he spent time with his family. How, to Bardo's disappointment, his military fatigues were nowhere to be found and he looked, except for the beard, and acted like any of the other visitors. "Have you heard about it from anyone else?"

"Actually," he says, "I have not been clear on whether it was a US surveillance base for listening to terrorist chatter or drug dealers' cell phones or a site for testing missiles or a radar station or a mirage. If you've been doing the disinformation, you are very, very good at it. I guess you didn't invite too many other third world commies like me, people who would give me the low down or confirm what Fidel said."

Bardo is smiling. Marley laughs at this. Then Bardo turns serious. "If you want to come to desde Desdemona, we need you to agree to two primary things. First, you have to promise to keep our island a secret from all of outsiders, and second, you have to state that you want to come with us. We can't take you there unless you really want to come and affirmatively say so. Because we make all decisions by consensus, that's what's required of us."

Acero nods. "I will discuss it with my family. I will tell you later today."

Bardo is wondering about whether the San Sebastian Liberation Front in exile might be a threat to desde Desdemona's tranquility and whether there is anything left of the SSLF for Acero to give up. If there's no San Sebastian and the entire population is scattered, there's no San Sebastian government to oppose. Will Acero want to create an opposition in desde Desdemona, where there isn't one, so he can oppose things? What is there in desde Desdemona to oppose anyway? Bardo marvels: he doesn't know what could be opposed. How do you oppose something that let's you do whatever you want?

Marley is fidgeting. He has more mundane concerns. He blurts it out. "It might be none of my business, but I want to ask you something about your life."

Acero's sudden smile is enormous. "Those stories, the ones about me and infidelities with a certain movie star. The photographs of us on the beach in Cuba. The videos of us at the Caribbean Conference in Panama City. Is she fantastic looking? Those were all made up. They are tabloid crap. Don't you recognize it as disinformation? She and I went to college together in the US, and are good friends. But the stories are all completely untrue, an attempt to discredit me on my island. On my island you don't fool around on your spouse. Period. Are you disappointed that you will probably not meet her?"

Marley doesn't want to admit that he's disappointed. He was wondering how the fabled, often chronicled public romance might continue in desde Desdemona, and whether the privacy of desde Desdemona and the lack of paparazzi would destroy the excitement of the affair he supposed was on going. Marley is more than slightly disappointed by this denial.

"But," Acero is saying, "When you see my wife, you will not be disappointed." Marley doesn't fully understand this remark. But it serves as a catalyst. Marley's mind sprints back to the flight to Barbados. He realizes that it'll be a while before Acero makes up his mind, and that there is a news story he is very interested in seeing closely.

*   *   *   *

"The story," the man in the tie is shouting, "The story is international cooperation in evacuating an island ravaged by a volcano, and that's what you must report. You must report that there is a coalition."

"You want me to ignore the arrest of Acero, the arrest of his family, the US helicopter that took him away, and the current situation?" Mari Estrella says with undisguised contempt, pointing to ships bobbing the harbor. She is standing under a tree at the docks. "Are we making a commercial for the transnationals or are we reporting the news? I'm not willing to sanitize this or tell the lies you demand."

"The story," the man continues, "Is solely the cooperation. Nobody gives a damn about the politics of an island nation that no longer exists. The current situation," he sweeps his hand at the boats, "is just a delay in off loading refugees. It is nothing more."

"You talking about this sit down demonstration?" She points again to the decks of two boats bobbing at anchor and the refugees, men, women, and children, sitting on the decks in direct sun, refusing to move. "They're not moving until they know that Acero is free and safe. The others will cover the story. We're going to look stupid and corrupt if we don't. Like liars and apologists. Like stooges for the power to the North."

The man exhales audibly, turns his back, and walks toward the sea muttering about women, stubbornness, and insubordination. At this, the camera man zooms in on Estrella's face and says, "Go ahead. Let's do your story while we still can."

"International cooperation in the evacuation of San Sebastian today was overshadowed by the arrest and apparent deportation of Manuel Acero, leader of the opposition San Sebastian Liberation Front, the main left-wing party in the island country. According to eyewitnesses, Acero and his family were arrested at gunpoint this morning at their home in Johnstown, transported to a US helicopter, and flown to an unknown destination.

"As news of Acero's arrest spread through the island's population, all of whom are being evacuated from the island because of the eruption of a volcano in the mountains of San Sebastian, various sit down strikes began on ships transporting the refugees to Barbados, from which they will be relocated to other islands.

"At this time, in the harbor of Bridgetown, at least two ships are lying at anchor with refugees from San Sebastian sitting down in protest on their decks.

The refugees reportedly are refusing to move until the whereabouts and condition of Acero are revealed.

"Acero is best known for his passionate denunciations of US influence in San Sebastian. He has described his eclectic brand of politics as Pina Colada Socialism because it was powerful and very easy to accept. Mari Estrella, Trans Caribe News, Barbados."

When Marley reaches the dock, there are cables everywhere, and the Bajans are standing four deep to watch the boats, police, refugees from San Sebastian, and the news people mix together like a conch stew. Various television news stations have satellite equipment spread on the ground, but he can't find the one person he has come to see. "Where on earth could she go?" he wonders. Then he sees her under the tree with the lights on her face, talking to the camera, and he sees the boats bobbing in the harbor.

As soon as the lights are off, a man in a tie approaches her. He is gesturing wildly, shouting something Marley can't hear. Estrella is not backing down and is arguing back. Marley realizes that he is not witnessing a simple professional disagreement about minor details, but something much more monumental. He also realizes that for the second time today he has to communicate with Mari, that the opportunity to be with her appears to be waning. He takes out a pad and pencil and he writes: "Dear Mari Estrella: If you can really keep a secret, and promise to do so, I would like you to come home to desde Desdemona with me later today. You can visit for however long you'd like. I am in the parking lot under a tree. Marley." He folds up the note, hands it to the camera man, makes sure that he will hand it to her, and walks to the parking lot. There he buys a mango from a fruit vendor, sits down on a bench under a tree in the shade and begins to eat it.

About 20 minutes later, as the mango's juice is dry on his hands and the thought that she's not coming home to desde Desdemona with him after all is becoming more prominent, Marley looks up. He sees Mari, the laptop and the sack of mangoes in her arms. "I just got fired," she says matter of factly. "I bet you know where Manuel Acero is."

"You have to promise me you will not tell about desde Desdemona" he says.

"Yes," she says, "Yes, I say yes."

Marley thinks Barbados hasn't much in common with Dublin.

*   *   *   *

The authorities in Barbados are "requesting" just one more "small favor" before Bardo and Marley can leave. The sit down strike on the two vessels has spread to the refugees on land, all of whom have decided to sit down in solidarity. The opposition party in Barbados is passing out handbills calling for a general strike if Acero's well being is not assured by 5 pm and urging Bajans to join in the demonstrations. Politicians, left and right, seize the TV and radio spotlight to grandstand: interventionist human rights violations throughout the Caribbean must not be countenanced, the Government and the UN should immediately undertake a complete inquiry about Acero's whereabouts. Faced with what appears to be an intractable confrontation, the authorities "small favor" is that Acero must address the demonstrators, show them he's well, and tell them peacefully to disperse.

Acero approaches the hastily constructed platform at the docks, and a hush falls over the huge crowd. The hum of the loudspeakers is the only sound. SSLF flags, red, black, green, and yellow stripes appear in the crowd. As Acero climbs the steps to the platform, the crowd immediately rises, fists thrust in the air, shouting "Acero, Acero, Acero." The chant is rhythmic, and there is clapping and drumming. The crowd begins a shimmering dance to the chant. As the crowd dances, tears flow. At last, Acero taps the microphone and the crowd falls silent again. The hum of the loudspeakers is again the only sound.

"Comrades and friends. Our lovely island home has been suddenly and forcefully reclaimed by nature. And all of us must now scatter to save ourselves and our families and to begin anew. We bring with us the few material possessions we have been able to salvage from San Sebastian. And our hearts and souls are the last repositories of the truth, idealism, power and yearning that grew from the harsh realities of our lives on San Sebastian into our beloved San Sebastian Liberation Front. Our wonderful island, and our deeply loved party no longer exist. We are to scatter like seeds driven by a hurricane. Wherever we may now land and plant our roots, let us retain within us the germ of our love of San Sebastian and our party. Wherever we go, may we firmly plant our roots and grow into tall trees that stand for justice, for freedom, for self determination. May we always be a stout tree sheltering the oppressed and protecting against exploitation. May we always link arms in solidarity with others, across the Caribbean and the world, to create a just and plentiful and rewarding life for all people.

"I am not going to Elba or Siberia. I am not going to prison or confinement. I am not being forced by the global multinationals and their surrogates to do anything. I and my family are going instead into a new privacy that we have chosen. We, like you, will now find and build a new home. We are all well and are not worthy of your further concern. Instead, we beseech each of you to recommit to the ideals of our island and our party, and to be a powerful force, wherever you may go, for justice and freedom and self determination.

"I and my family wish you all well. May we all find new homes, and may we all continue to stand for what is right. Goodbye, and Viva SSLF."

At this the crowd immediately rises as one and begins to chant and dance "Viva Acero, Viva SSLF." A tear runs down Acero's cheek as he backs away from the microphones. He raises his right arm in a clenched fist salute.

CHAPTER 7

▼

At Estrella's request, the yellow sea plane circles the volcano on San Sebastian on its flight to desde Desdemona. An evasive course is not required this once because of the pay back for the two "small favors." The smoke is thick and billows from the center of the island. Acero and his family stare sullenly out the window, looking for their former home. Then Acero says, "Good bye." His wife and his three kids begin quietly to cry. Acero's lip quivers, and a tear emerges on his eye lid. The passengers in the plane fall silent.

After a while, Estrella breaks the silence. "Do you think it will be easy to give up your very public life for the very private, the very secret life you're now beginning?" The question surprisingly does not seem out of place. Maybe it's because of the softness of Estrella's voice.

Acero stares into space. There is a wetness on his eyes that sparkles. Then he begins slowly and softly, "My work on San Sebastian is now finished. Because the island is finished, not because we won or because we lost. I'm sure that a next thing for me to do will emerge. Until it does, for the meanwhile, I want to sit quietly in the sun. I want to regroup. I want to smell the salt from the sea and watch the birds. Maybe I will fish. I want to sleep without worries waking me up in the middle of the night. I want to day dream. I want to read good novels. If you pardon my saying so, I want to make love in the middle of the day and be uninterrupted. I would like to take a nap on Sunday afternoons. Are these strange thoughts for a revolutionary? If my life were a string of beads, you could think of this flight as connecting two beads. The beads are related by the string, they're not identical. Who knows what surprises and jewels I will find in this next bead with time, solitude, reflection, peace."

Acero turns to look out the window at the turquoise sea below him. He begins to hum to himself. It is a tune he learned as a child about the flag of Puerto Rico, the beautiful flag of Puerto Rico. It goes round and round in his humming. It is oddly comforting. "La bonita bandera, la bonita bandera, la bandera Puerto Ricana..."

Estrella also watches the sea, the small waves, the glinting diamonds at the tips of waves. She begins to ponder the relationship of faith to Marxist historical determinism, but loses her thread when she notices that Marley is looking at her. He is handsome, charming, off beat. The thought arises that she doesn't really know him. She is surprised that it doesn't seem to matter. She is drawn to him anyway. She notices that she likes the shape of his hands and fingers, and that she is not angry that she no longer has a job. No, there is no anger. She feels a kind of surprising relief and a joyful, mildly intoxicating excitement. She smiles at him. Yes, she thinks, she is happy with this surprising, sudden change in her life. Very unexpected, she thinks. I couldn't have predicted this this morning, but I'm quite happy. Quite happy, thank you.

*   *   *   *

Oscar is fascinated with Swamiji. They seem to have nothing substantive to say to each other, but they always smile at each other and nod. Oscar clearly enjoys watching Swamiji. He marvels at the things Swamiji tells Arjuna to do, eat nothing but watermelon, drink gallons of water, eat nothing but vegetables, drink nothing but water with lemon juice, and on and on. He loves to hear Swamiji cackle and laugh. And he is astonished that Arjuna, who previously argued incessantly with the realities of his daily existence, faithfully, albeit humorlessly does exactly whatever he is told. What, he wonders, is Arjuna trying to accomplish? Is this the road to what he calls enlightenment? Maybe, thinks Oscar, something will happen that will get all of this to make sense. When it happens, I will know that it is because of Arjuna's persistence and his listening to what Swamiji says. Only I can't imagine what it will look like. Will there be a sudden, a dramatic change? Maybe if he laughed along, things would go easier for him. Maybe if the journey were being enjoyed it would pass with greater ease. Time, Oscar thinks, will eventually reveal everything.

Meanwhile, from a ramp high in the trees, Swamiji has been watching Oscar's floating naps with great interest. One afternoon, when it is particularly hot and the sea is extremely still and mirror like, Swamiji drops his robe on the beach and swims out to where Oscar is floating.

"Not disturbing you, am I?" Swamiji asks him.

"Not at all. I'm surprised to find you here. I thought you stayed on land and told people what to eat."

Swamiji starts to laugh at this, then realizing that he wants the water to remain calm and undisturbed, suppresses the laughter. He rolls over on his back, floating, imitating Oscar. They float silently together for about twenty minutes.

"When you float on your back, do you always hear your breathing?" Swamiji asks.

"It's very relaxing to listen to it. You also hear the shells moving up and down the beach under the waves, rolling up and down the beach with the tide. And, if you pay attention and are lucky, you can sometimes hear the dolphins talking. When that happens, you sometimes receive pictures from them."

"What are the pictures like?"

"Forgive me if I sound a lot like you," Oscar says, "But you have to receive the pictures yourself to understand this. I can't really explain it. But I'm sure you will be here at the right time for that. The dolphins are very generous with their pictures, and it helps if you let them know you would like pictures from them. I don't have to tell you that, though, right?"

Soon, Swamiji and his disciples were floating together off the reef in the morning and the evening. The disciples, who previously seemed to overlook him, were trying repeatedly to make eye contact with Oscar. They may have been hoping that he would speak to them. But, of course, Oscar had nothing to say that he thought the disciples would consider to be of substance. And Swamiji, they noticed, seemed to be spending more and more time beside Oscar. This, of course, made the disciples seek Oscar's eyes even more, hoping for an all important, enlightening communication from him.

*   *   *   *

The children, who despite Ona's desires have been glued to the television watching the evacuation, have decided to welcome Acero and his family with a ceremony. They will convey the Acero family to desde Desdemona in a century old log canoe originally owned by Oscar and Milagros, and rumored to be the vessel they originally used to flee Guyana. Of course, Acero's assent to this is unnecessary; the canoe will end up being the only unoccupied vessel when the sea plane lands. The idea, according to Jeremy, is that if newcomers arrive the same way as the original founders, they have the same connection to desde Desdemona and there is no difference between new arrivals and the original ones except time.

All time, Jeremy and Swamiji and most people on Desde Desdemona believe, is utterly simultaneous. Everything is happening at the same time. The past and the future happen along with the present, moment by simultaneous moment. The present, the past, the future are different stories and are all happening right now.

When the propellers have stopped and the yellow sea plane has silently glided close to the beach, the rafts, canoes, surfboards, rowboats, and the century old dugout all bob at its pontoons. Acero appears at the door, helping his family into the dugout. He is smiling. He thinks desde Desdemona is even more extremely beautiful than he had heard, and that Fidel was a fool to go back to Cuba, its rotting 1950s automobiles, its sugar cane, the unjust US embargo and its resultant economic struggle. I should have believed Fidel about this, Acero thinks. The children see him, and imitating what they saw earlier in the day on television, briefly chant, "Viva Acero, Viva SSLF." But the chant doesn't catch on and it fades away on the breeze. Instead, the adults wave and call out, "Welcome, Welcome to desde." Acero and his wife wave; their children are silent as the flotilla slowly tows the canoe to the beach. When Acero and his family exit the dugout, children hand them fruit and wreaths of white jasmine flowers and shake their hands. Jeremy and Rosa somehow convince the Acero children to run off with them.

In the crowd John Coltrane Ramirez shakes his head. "There's only one guy, and to me it doesn't look like he's exactly an antelope. He's another stinking midfielder I bet. I'm going to have to get help elsewhere. That damn volcano is a disaster through and through."

"Well," Marley says as he and Bardo secure the plane. "We've been left behind. We're going to have to wade." Bardo shrugs. "What did you expect? We always wade, don't we?"

At this Estrella returns her laptop to the floor of the plane, hefts the sack of mangoes and her small back pack, and grabbing Marley by the arm, jumps from the pontoon into the sea, pulling Marley into the water backwards. He lands with a splash, then stands up sputtering and laughing. He removes the baseball cap, dumping the water from it, grinning, his dreadlocks dripping. "You wild woman!" he laughs. "I know you're going to like desde Desdemona." He gives her a hug. "Welcome," he says. Then, backing slightly away from her, he trips her with his right leg, gives her a push at the shoulders, and watches as she falls backwards, splashing into the sea. She emerges laughing, hugs him tight to her with both arms, and plants a delicious, salt water kiss on his mouth.

*   *   *   *

At the last palm tree before the beach, Oscar is building a small altar. He intends it to be shaped like a bird house and to hang at eye level from the tree. It must, however, not harm the tree in any way. Arjuna sees him working, planing wood, fastening it together, building a harness to go around the trunk of the tree, holding pieces of wood up to the tree to see how it should look. He sees that it will be an altar, and thinks, "Where will he get a statue? Maybe he brought one back from one of the nearby Catholic islands and has been saving it." Arjuna, however, does not stop to talk; hungry and searching for the ripe avocados he has been instructed to eat exclusively, he grunts hello and, absorbed in the search for the acceptable, right food, trudges on.

Something Swamiji has told Oscar has captivated him. Sailors in far away India, he has learned, are devoted to the goddess called Green Tara. This manifestation of the heavenly mother, Swamiji says, guides people safely across the ocean of illusion to arrive at the shore of enlightenment. The sailors venerate the goddess because they are crossing actual oceans and need to find the beach safely. How like me, Oscar is thinking. How like my journey with Milagros to desde Desdemona. How perfect a journey, when we had no known destination, to arrive on these shores and find a home. I want to express my gratitude for this to Green Tara. It must have been she who extended her grace to us and was responsible for seeing to our safety, for sending us the dolphins. Perhaps I will find something suitable to place inside her shrine. For now, building this altar to show her my gratitude is a good beginning.

After completing the altar, Oscar, finding nothing to place in it, kneels before the empty shrine and prays out loud, "Thank you for showing us grace. Thank you for our long, safe journey and peaceful arrival. Thank you for providing us with such a beautiful and fertile home. My intention is to honor and praise you." He stands and thinks, "Something will show up. I will talk with Milagros and see what she recommends." There is a feeling of comfort, Oscar notices, from building the altar and directly stating his thanks.

That night, Oscar has a dream. In it a huge, green sea turtle lumbers onto the dark beach of desde Desdemona. It is low tide and the full moon glistens on its carapace. It sparkles like a bejeweled crown. The tortoise slowly digs a hole and methodically buries its eggs. But instead of returning to the sea as the tide rises, she floats on the shallow waves inland, struggling further up the beach, toward the tree line, away from the deep water. In his dream, Oscar runs toward her through the shallow water and calls out to her, "Go back, go back. You'll be grounded. You've got to turn around and go back toward the sea." He tries to push her shell back down the beach, but he cannot move her. His heart is pounding with the exertion. She raises her head, and she says to him in a very slow, very deep, rich bass voice, "You know me. I am the embodiment of compassion. You have found me and I have found you. You are living on my back in harmony with my beings. Continue to honor me by cultivating your compassion for all beings; I am protecting you." His eyes fill with tears, he awakes sobbing. He wakes Milagros, telling her something terrible is happening. They hurry to the beach together.

When they arrive it is full high tide. The entire beach is under water. There is no turtle. Oscar cries out, "Thank God! In my dream I forgot that the beach gets completely flooded. Oh Thank God!" He hugs Milagros, and begins again to sob deeply.

In the morning at the low tide, Oscar finds a small, brass statue of Green Tara nestled in the shrine. It is clothed in moist, green seaweed. He cannot understand its arrival. Again, his tears flow down his face. He kneels before the altar, bows deeply to the sand, and again speaks his thanks for his long, safe journey, for his magnificent home, and for the mystery his gratitude has revealed.

$$* \qquad * \qquad * \qquad *$$

Mari is sitting on Marley's deck. Her laptop is in front of her. The screen saver makes idiotic, continuous plumbing configurations. Underneath, the word processing screen is blank. She can barely hear the machine's insect like thrumming. She has tentatively decided two things. First, she will stay with Marley, whom she believes she loves, and see how their relationship continues to develop. And second, she will try to write a short novel about desde Desdemona. Not War and Peace. Not the Brothers K. Not 100 Years of Solitude. Just something short that conveys the richness and peace she has found in this remarkable place. Ok, a novella. Maybe even a long short story. Marley is delighted about both ideas. He gently reminds her about the promise of secrecy she made him. And he reminds her that she has also promised a story to the children. Mari has finished that; would Marley like to be the first to hear the story? Would he like a private reading?

*   *   *   *

"Once upon a time in a country with palm trees and a turquoise sea, there lived a fisherman. He had not always lived by fishing, and his home had not always had palm trees surrounding it. Many years before he was a poet, employed in a city where trees lost their leaves and rivers turned to ice. This is the story of how he became a fisherman.

"One day the poet awoke early. It was a Thursday like any other. He had to go to town to buy bread and onions. And he had to write a poem. A poem filled with rhymes and the sounds of howling wolves and the stillness of falling snow and images of the faint blue light cast by a frozen star. This poem he would bring to the prince on Friday and read to the Prince's Court.

"All the rich and powerful men would nod at how well he commanded the language and how clever he was. And the hearts of the beautiful and rich ladies would beat a little faster and a slight blush would come to their faces at the depth of his sensitivity and the glimpse he gave them of his passion for life.

"The poet went to town and bought bread and onions. He did this because the onions symbolized the depth of earth and the surprises he lived by. And the bread symbolized the magic he loved, the yeast mysteriously turning dry flour and water to rich crusty bread. He put the onions to boil for soup and sat in his chair to write the poem.

"But alas, after 2 or 3 hours of patiently waiting, no poem came to him. Had the muse of his poetry gone on vacation? Was the poet within him on strike? Had someone picked all of the poems off his poem tree while he slept? What was wrong? He had no idea what was the matter.

"The poet became afraid. What would the rich and powerful men and the rich and beautiful ladies say if he had no poem? Worse yet, what of the prince who depended on his poems to inspire his guests and to impress them with beauty?

"He began to think of the ice, the deep black ice of lakes, and how the geese returning in early Spring sighed disappointment when they could not land on water and wheeled in the sky to slide onto the ice. He thought of the wind, sharp as a razor, and how it lashed the faces and froze the beards and brought tears to the eyes that froze like diamonds on the tips of eyelashes. He thought of the wails of wolves as they cried at the blue sun for warmth and water and green but huddled instead in their frozen holes, hungry, to wait and dream of a new season. He could not find a single poem in any of this.

"Instead, his heart spoke to him of blue seas and hot suns, that somewhere, far away in a distant country, there was always fruit on the trees and no need for coats and no real need for fire or quilts or heavy woolen cloth or skins. Could he tell this poem to the prince and the Court? Would they banish him? After all, it was his charge to write a northern winter poem for a northern winter prince and a northern winter court.

"Then a smile came to his face and immediately a poem appeared on the paper before him:

I stand on a white beach,
A hot sun and a turquoise sea
Filled with fish before me.
The blue sun, howls of wolves
Are a distant almost forgotten
Memory. And snow has never been
Dreamt of here.
I am a poet who can turn small
Children to sparrows. But I could
Not melt the black ice of lakes
And I could not make the frozen rivers
Flow.
But I could dream of the
Place, far away, where
There is always fruit and
Fishermen need no shoes.

"When he finished reading this poem, instead of the usual applause and cheers and shouts of delight, there was a great, deep, cavernous silence. You could hear a distant clock tick.

"Eventually, the prince, wearing rich ermine, rose and spoke. 'These are thoughts that are forbidden in this country because they make us weaker in the face of extreme winter. The usual penalty for such speech is death. But I will spare this poet because of his many years of service, and I order him to be banished to the land he dreams of. May no further mention of this evening be made on penalty of death.'

"As he stood before his home on a beach with palm trees and a turquoise sea, the prince's speech was only a distant memory, as was the four month sea voyage and its many ports, each one warmer than its predecessor. A smile came to his browned face, and he laughed out loud."

CHAPTER 8

▼

Oscar is shaving. He is completely naked. He is bending his nose over to the left, so that it is out of the way of the straight razor, and he is talking to Milagros as he goes. He knocks the lather off the razor over the railing and into the sea below. It floats in the air on its descent. "So I have invited Swamiji and his gang to eat with us. I have no idea why his gang is so interested in me, but since we caught such a large fish this morning, I thought we could feed all of them well. Maybe you can help me discover why they look at me so intently."

Milagros is standing close behind him. She has a long handled clipper in her hand, and some cuttings from a plant. "Maybe it's because you are so sexy and strong." She pats him on the buttock. He is surprisingly hard and muscular. "Or because of your dreaming of Green Tara and making the altar. Who knows what foolishness Swamiji may have told them about you, or for that matter about me."

Oscar starts to laugh. "It must be about you, my beauty. They must wonder what secret spiritual magic I possess for someone as beautiful and talented as you to be my wife and lover. They want me to tell them my secret aphrodisiacs." He starts to giggle. "You know, they are quite interested in matters of love. Lisette reports that Swamiji's gang think a lot about making love, mostly with people they knew years and years, even decades ago, before they put on robes and made their promises of celibacy. They forget to cross their fingers behind their backs. And then they feel bad about thinking unchaste thoughts. Their vow, it seems to them, extends to the normal operations of their minds as well. Lisette says that's because once they embark on their path, they believe they're not supposed to think about sex any more. It's not supposed to arise, if you'll forgive me. They certainly don't ever tell Swamiji that they're thinking so frequently about love making. Lisette and the other dolphins find this idea that they're supposed to not have these thoughts hysterically funny and uniquely human. She has asked Swamiji several times to relieve them from their misconceptions about thoughts about lovemaking. But he just laughs whenever she tells him about this. He says he has never told them not to think about lovemaking. And he insists that he never told them of anything else not to think about either. That, he says, would be silly. Thoughts, he has told them, are just thoughts. You observe them but don't hold them and they fly away like pollen. You hold tightly onto them and they grow roots and branches and expand. They become trees."

"I will make some spicy mango chutney to go with the grilled fish. I know they will enjoy this. Some of these people might even secretly believe that eating spicy food gives rise to desire and diverts them from an ascetic path to enlightenment. This gang follows Swamiji, so they all eat spicy food, don't they?" She is smiling. "The food is probably the least of the reasons why they're always thinking about lovemaking." Her smile turns into a laugh.

"Swamiji's thoughts have been a real gift to the dolphins," Oscar adds. "Lisette says his thoughts are crystal clear, that he constantly feels and expresses his appreciation for the world and this island. When he is floating and dreaming in the sea, he has given her pictures of extremely tall, craggy, snow covered mountains, lakes that glisten like mirrors, and huge vistas. In the vistas are monuments, flags that blow in the wind, enormous long haired cow-like animals, and the monuments and stones and rocks have prayers etched and carved all over them. In these pictures the air is very thin, the sun is always extremely bright even though it is often cold, and the clouds are like fluffy pillows. Swamiji also fondly remembers all his teachers and praises them for their guidance to him. His dreams are filled with his appreciation, prayers and thanksgiving. The dolphins treasure him and these dreams. They pass these dreams around to each other and discuss them and savor them."

*   *   *   *

Ona, Carmen Acero, and Mari Estrella sit in chairs near the beach in a shady grove. Flowering boughs shake gently overhead in the breeze, gently scenting the air. The orange flowers attract bees and humming birds. In the distance is the faint roar of waves crossing the reef. "I'm here officially to welcome you to desde Desdemona and to help you with your transition," Ona says. She offers each of them mineral water and sliced mango and papaya and lime. "It's an easy task for you and your families. All you have to do is put on these orange bracelets." The bracelets are made of a single strand of orange glass beads with a shiny fastener. "People wearing no bracelets are working. Tourists know that they can ask them for anything and be served. The orange means that you're not tourists—they wear yellow bracelets—when you wear them, it means you're not working and that you reside here. That this is your home and a day off." Estrella smiles and colors slightly at the idea of being a resident and having a home in desde Desdemona. Ona smiles at her. "So, for the next two weeks or so you act like tourists, get to know the island and the people who live here, and all of us will give you our best tourist treatment. That means we'll arrange whatever you want. As they say in Trinidad, 'We'll arrange to suit.'

"The best transitional advice is to do exclusively whatever you feel like whenever you feel like it. That's what most of us do here anyway. If you want to, make full use of the massage and other relaxation services. Go diving and snorkeling and fishing. Sit in the hot tub. Watch the birds and monkeys. Swim. Take day trips. Drink wine. Ask people who are working to do things for you. If you feel like doing nothing, do that. Our goal is to get you so relaxed that you forget what day of the week it is. We want you to get so unwound that you can't feel any outside world tension in your bodies. Use this time to explore what it's like not to be sleep deprived. Find out what it's like to live without ever looking at your watch. See if you lose that reflex to turn toward your wrist. If you like, you can forget about anything that's happening in the outer world; avoid newspapers and television if you would like to. You might put your watches away. Your cell phones won't work here. When you're thoroughly relaxed, and ready for something to do, we'll meet and, if you'd like, together we'll design your work. I know it sounds weird, and right now, is impossible to conceive of, but the day will probably come when you will want to be doing something that vaguely resembles work of some sort. If it doesn't come to that, that's entirely ok too. There is no pressure here.

"Carmen, your kids ran off with my Jeremy and Rosa and their friends. The kids are welcoming them. They, I'm sure, are having a wonderful time. They're safe. Kids love it here. So do their parents. After all, every single person living on this island is dedicated to making it paradise for everyone here, including themselves."

Carmen smiles at this idea, that Ona said "including themselves". Ona notices that Carmen is extremely beautiful, that she is wearing dangling earrings with bits of feather in them, and that there is a bright shine in her eyes. She gazes in Carmen's eyes; Carmen gazes back. In the instant there is a spark of recognition that marks the beginning of an understanding. Ona thinks, "This is a wise, powerful woman. She is so familiar to me." Carmen thinks, "She is remarkable. Where could I know her from?"

Mari notices these glances. She wonders about the net of connections between the people in desde and how strong its fabric is. How, she wonders, is this community bound together? There must be friction and disruption and hostility. I haven't seen them yet, she thinks, but they have to be here. Or do they? There have to be arguments, don't there? They're human, so they must make messes. I wonder where all of that is. They cannot have gotten beyond that.

"Oh," Ona interrupts the silence. "I almost forgot. There is a very special event that might happen tonight. The giant green sea turtles are about to lay their eggs. They come up on the beach on full moon nights at low tide, dig holes, and plant their eggs. Then they return to the water. If you want us to wake you to see them in the moonlight—they're on the endangered species list—just let me know. The coming of the turtles marks a very special event in the history and life of this island. When they come, we have a special festival and a thanksgiving holiday."

*   *   *   *

Arjuna falls asleep to the sound of the birds and insects. The hammock swings slightly, his breath deepens, his eyelids become heavy. Soon he is dreaming. In his dream it is night. He hears splashing coming from the beach, and he hears Oscar's voice shouting. He runs through the trees to the beach, he constantly trips on the roots of trees and on bushes. He stubs his feet, he falls down and gets up to run again. Branches and vines tear at his arms, face and chest. When he finally arrives he is panting and his hands and chest and legs and feet are scraped and sore and bleeding. The full moon is shining on the sea, and he sees Oscar standing in a foot of water pleading and pushing something. He comes closer and sees that there is an enormous green sea turtle. Its back is covered in sharp, grey barnacles, and Oscar's hands are cut and bleeding from pushing on it. Oscar is shouting for the turtle to go back, to return from the beach to the sea, but he can't budge the creature, and his hands and arms are red with his blood. Oscar cries out, "Go back, go back. You'll be grounded. You've got to turn around and go back." He tries to push her shell back down the beach, but he cannot move her and his hands are ripped by the barnacles with each attempt. Arjuna's heart is pounding. Saying nothing, he takes off his shirt and pants and offers them to Oscar, to wrap around his hands. As soon as these are tied on Oscar's hands, the turtle wheels toward the sea, pushes once with her huge legs, and smoothly slides down the beach, disappearing silently into the deep water. The waters part and she is enfolded in them. Arjuna is naked. He cries out in desperation, "Wait. Stop. I want to see you. I need to see you. I know who you are. Come back to me. Come back!" But it is too late, the massive turtle is gone. Oscar and he are both sobbing.

Arjuna is jolted awake by this dream. He is crying. His heart is breaking open. In his chest and solar plexus is a deep canyon brimming with an enormous ocean of sadness. How like my grasping for enlightenment are Oscar's cut hands, he thinks. The thought increases his sobs, his body is wracked with crying. I'm always working against myself, and it's exhausting. I'm hurting myself. I'm making myself bleed. He pulls on clothes. I need to believe in and receive grace or there's no change. His body is drenched in sweat and tears; the clothing sticks to him. Sobbing deeply, he touches Saraswati's shoulder, says he is going to Swamiji's, and scuttles down the deck in the dark. Arjuna's only thought is that Swamiji has something to tell him, that he must immediately go to Swamiji. It is the middle of the night. The moon is bright, and the palm trees rattle in the breeze. In the distance, lightning intermittently illuminates the insides of several clouds, but it does not strike the ground.

Saraswati sits up in the hammock. Her thought is that something wonderful is happening and that Arjuna has just broken through. It is as if an open window suddenly appeared in the midst of a solid brick wall and the breeze could enter. She smiles in gratitude. She notices that things seem perfect to her. She realizes that she has been waiting.

*   *   *   *

Marley is playing some of his favorite music for Mari Estrella. Actually, he is playing the same 16 bars over and over and over again. He jokes that he missed his true vocation by living on desde Desdemona, that he could have had a wonderful career in the US or South America translating music lyrics from English into Spanish. He demonstrates his knack for rendering an indecipherable blues mumble first into English and then into Spanish. Urged on to new heights, he then translates the old spiritual, "Cuando Dios es listo, tienes que muever. You gotta move."

"Is that what he said?"

"Absolutely."

"You're sure?"

"Absolutely. Listen to it again. This is gonna completely change your understanding of music. It's gonna open up a whole new world. The world of lyrics. These guys are actually saying something."

"But that's why they sometimes print the words inside the box. And sometimes you're not supposed to understand the words anyway, right?"

"Nobody reads that stuff. Most people don't even know it's there. People of a certain age can't even open the boxes. They have their kids do it. Then they lose the boxes." He folds his hands on his heart. Then he starts to hum the tune, "When the Lord gets ready, you got to move."

Bardo arrives on the deck carrying some papers. "Let him finish. Why do you keep playing the same phrase over and over again?"

"Look at this," he says, handing Marley People magazine.

Marley stares at the half page photograph. His mouth is open. He hands the magazine to Mari. "What's the problem? Acero is kind of like Elvis, he's disappeared after Barbados and nobody knows where he's gone. So they run a picture of him and his wife—doesn't she look elegant in this gown?—and ask, 'What has happened to the photogenic darling of pina colada socialism and Carmen, his wife? Has he, like President Mobutu, cashed in and gone into seclusion in France?' And then they dutifully report the rumors that he is somewhere in Europe, probably the south of France or Monaco, or in South America, or Rarotonga. They have narrowed the search, it seems, to three continents and a vast expanse of ocean, to places within 15,000 kilometers of each other."

"The problem," Bardo says, "is that on the heels of this article, television crews from the US networks are already in Barbados looking for his trail. And we don't want them to arrive here. Remember your ancestor and what a mess that first photograph of Milagros made? This might be a replay of that. Let's meet later and make a plan."

"It's too bad that they are not being left alone. I like her," Estrella says. "Has Acero seen the article?"

Bardo nods. "He was out fishing for tarpon or bonefish with a fly rod. He says he thinks his wife's appearance is the only reason the media ever paid any attention to him. That it certainly wasn't the excitement and magnetism of his campaign for economic justice and freedom on a tiny island like San Sebastian. San Sebastian, Acero says, could have been another Grenada, invaded by the US because they didn't like the indigenous brand of left wing politics, if his wife had not made him appear charismatic. Her beauty, he says, and her love for him kept him and his movement alive. It made his movement more like a movie than real life. More charismatic. People admired them as a couple, even when there were ugly rumors and disinformation. If she had not been thoroughly photogenic, and always in the public eye, and ready to help his struggle, he would, he thought, have ended up like Che."

Marley finds this disturbing. He cannot remember the name of the former president of Grenada. He can only remember the name of the deposed president of Haiti. Ending up like Che, he thinks, is not what anyone has planned.

*　　*　　*　　*

Arjuna finds Swamiji sitting on a brown reed floor mat meditating. A small candle is burning. There is nag champa incense smoke. The only sound is the tide breaking below the deck, the sound of wind and wave against the reef, the clattering of palm trees, and some howler monkeys bellowing at each other in the distance. As he reaches to touch Swamiji's shoulder, Swamiji softly says, "Sit down next to me. Close your eyes." Arjuna sits. He immediately starts to tremble from head to foot. It's 27 degrees Celsius; he's freezing.

Arjuna trembles for many minutes. His breathing is spasmodic. At last Swamiji speaks so softly that Arjuna has to strain to hear his words, "You have just experienced a taste of the perfection and grace in all things including you. There is nothing to do but to appreciate it and to feel and express your gratitude for her grace to the goddess who protected you on the sea, brought you here, gave you a home, fulfilled your wishes, and came to you even in your dreaming to show you a joyful path, the path of ease and love to the goal you say you are seeking. She is showing you that the path and the goal are the same. You are already there but don't let it be realized. Now you can realize it."

Swamiji resumes his silence. Slowly, Arjuna's trembling abates, but his mind picks up the shaking and begins to rattle and lurch and tremble in thoughts, analyses, comparisons, judgments, inquiries, and voices. In the midst of all of this, he notices something brand new, that deep inside him he feels delight and that he is profoundly thankful for the experience of it. The delight is initially just a small yellow flickering that emerges and then withdraws. When it's present, it sparkles briefly. Then it recedes, only to re-emerge stronger to his surprise and joy. It defies being held or touched. It dances in and out of his awareness just beyond his control. To him it is a taste of all occupying bliss. Tears roll down his face. He is content. He has never been so thoroughly and completely happy. He breathes easily, and marvels at the depth of his relaxation.

When Arjuna finally opens his eyes, the sun has risen. Swamiji has left. The candle has burned out. He walks slowly through the trees to the altar Oscar built, sits down, and offers prayers and thanksgiving to the mother Green Turtle. He places a small ripe mango on the edge of the altar at the feet of Green Tara, leaning it against the carved lotus on which the goddess sits. There is nothing else to say or do or think or feel. He feels the sand under this feet and the breeze on his forehead and hears the tide. "Thank you," he says out loud. "Thank you. Thank you."

CHAPTER 9

▼

Marley, Bardo, Acero and Carmen stand neck deep in the turquoise sea. Bardo likes to call this spot on the south beach his office, Officina del Sur. There are small, sharp, incongruous needled cacti in the shade under the trees. And there are no waves. In the distance they can see the dolphins gliding across the surface and pelicans diving for their perpetual dinner. Beyond the dolphins and the birds, all the way to the horizon is unbroken, sparkling turquoise. They are discussing various alternatives.

Finally, Bardo says, "I agree we should do nothing at this time. If the TV people stay in Barbados for too much longer, you may need to appear briefly in France. Just long enough to get noticed and photographed. Maybe you can punch a photographer or something. Then you can disappear in a huff. After that, the news people will definitely leave Barbados and pick up your trail in France."

"If it comes to that, maybe you and Carmen can spend a couple of days in the Grand Hotel. You need to be seen together so they don't start more rumors. You're gonna be amazed at how filthy and crowded and polluted France and the Mediterranean is. You can have some time alone; you can visit with expatriate South American poets and such. Eat escargots, drink wine. Disapprove of bourgeouis casinos and mass media images. Belatedly endorse France's non-participation in the Iraq invasion. Complain about mistreatment of Algerians and other Muslims. Be seen. Get annoyed. Then we can pull you out of there without a trace. Of course, you'd have to be willing to keep desde Desdemona a complete secret. Would you be willing do this in the event that you have to?"

Acero looks at Carmen. She frowns, then exhales audibly. "I hope I don't have to go," she says. "I don't want those people tugging on me any more. I like being here, and desde Desdemona holds a wonderful future for us and our kids. I am feeling at home. I actually believe I might be able to have a new kind of life here. So if I don't have to go, and I really hope I don't, I want to stay disappeared as far as the outside world is concerned and become just another local here. They will soon forget about us, I hope. Isn't our 15 minutes up yet? Is that reasonable?"

Acero reaches out and takes her hand. They are both wearing orange bracelets. "I would like that for us," he says. "If we have to go to Europe, we will. Then we can return. It's only fair to protect the island that is now becoming our home. Personally, I'm not willing to appear on any of the cable news interview shows. I don't want to be interviewed. I don't want to be infotainment. That would be asking entirely too much. Other than that, I'll do it."

Carmen smiles. "We haven't changed, have we?" she says and cradles his hand in hers. She wonders about her willingness to be helpful. What would she be like if she just turned her back and refused to help? What an unthinkable, ugly way to behave, to leave others to suffer.

*   *   *   *

It is very late afternoon and Swamiji is falling asleep in the sea. The sun has scattered a field of diamonds across the water. He is floating on his back close to shore in very warm water. He is wondering about the altar Oscar built and how that may have been connected to Oscar's dream of Green Tara and to Arjuna's similar dream. Which of these are interrelated causes and which are results? What a silly question. He giggles. He savors Arjuna's nocturnal arrival and the mango Arjuna has left as an offering for Green Tara. His body hums with pleasure at the very idea. He is filled with the proximity of the heavenly mother. And he, too, recalls his gratitude to Her for his safe arrival and home on desde Desdemona. Her bliss envelopes him, and he basks in the glow of her compassion. His delight and comfort increase with each audible breath he takes. He has just begun to visualize the heavenly mother as the ancient, enormous green mother turtle, laden with eggs, her back green and brown and shining, when he hears the voice.

"Do not be afraid," she says in a very deep, slow voice that seems to surround him from deep underwater. His heart begins to pound, and the hair on his arms starts to stand on end, but he does not move. He returns to hearing his breathing and to listening deeply, patiently for her. His heart continues to pound. "I am the ancient mother of this island," she continues. "In my present body I am 154 years old. The generations of my children and grandchildren were born on this island, as were the generations of all my relations. I and my kin are a source of protection and compassion to the generations of dolphins who shelter and thrive here. I have appeared now to inspire you who have recently arrived and made your homes in this domain, on the ridge of my back, to preserve my paradise and to cultivate my peace and to cause a vast ocean of compassion to flourish. I am here to protect and guide you on your journeys." Swamiji's eyes are closed, but the sweetness and richness of her voice fills his eyes with tears. "There is no limitation to the power of compassion nor to the strength of peace. I am here whenever you may need me. You need only ask. I will visit others, too. You and they will strongly feel my presence. I am here for them also. I am always, always available to you." Swamiji continues to float. He has never been so comfortable. "You may ask for my help by coming to me or calling out to me. I will come. All is truly well here." Swamiji is wrapped in glorious comfort and he falls sound asleep. He is entirely buoyant and relaxed.

When he awakes, Swamiji has grounded himself on the beach. He has no idea how long his head has been parked on the sand. His body is still afloat. And his feet are wrinkled like prunes. The sun has gone down. It is dark. He walks up the beach toward the trees. There, under the tree with the altar, he sees, glistening in the moon light, the huge shell. He sees the gouge the shell has made in the sand and the enormous green turtle digging a hole with her flippers. He stands among the trees and watches. On the beach he sees some other female turtles pulling themselves out of the water, their shells sparkling with diamonds and rubies in the moon light. They too lumber toward the trees, gouging deep furrows in the sand, until they reach their chosen destinations. Then they too start to dig.

Swamiji feels awe and delight emerge from his heart. His eyes fill with tears. He is spellbound. His entire body is covered with goose bumps. He starts softly to repeat the mantra of Tara, "Om Tara Tuttare Ture Svaha." He sinks to his knees and clasps his hands together before his heart, then prostrates himself face down on the beach.

When he finally arises, he hears a sound to his left. He turns to see Oscar, Arjuna, Saraswati, and Milagros all on their knees on the beach. All have their eyes closed, tears stream down their faces, and their hands are clasped before their hearts. All have sand on their foreheads and chests. All are silent.

*   *   *   *

The Lemuria Times is desde Desdemona's twice weekly newspaper. It was founded in the early 1970s by former campus radicals who originally produced it just for fun and to re-experience the excitement of manic mimeographing. It was a combination of propaganda for New Left participatory democracy and hallucinatory discussions of the cosmos. They then sold it for 1 sonrise or gave it away on the beach. Originally, the newspaper attempted to provide an insightful, critical analysis of Caribbean events, but because so few of those events seemed to have any practical significance for life in desde Desdemona, and because word of mouth was so quick and detailed, the newspaper moved away from news to providing a uniquely laid back discussion of local and world events. The newspaper acknowledged that it was at most only a second source. The first source was gossip. Later, satellite television and the Internet made the newspaper at most a third source. Because of the Times's role in the life of desde Desdemona, a list of the moves made in chess games between the world chess champion and a computer, a humorous account of the local soccer game (making light of John Coltrane Ramirez's intensity), the English premier soccer league standings, a story about negotiations in fishing net treaties and a moratorium on fishing in New England, and a speech by the Dalai Lama were all given greater prominence than the arrivals of the Acero family and Mari Estrella. The newspaper carries no advertising and the bottom of the front page is entirely a list of events and a schedule of available activities. In fact, the arrival of Estrella, who the children had frequently seen on television, achieved slightly greater notice than the arrival of Acero, but neither received much play. The two sentence article tersely noted at the bottom of a column that Caribe Network reporter Mari Estrella, whose reports of the recent volcano were so informative, and a subject of those reports, the leader of the San Sebastian Liberation Front, Manuel Acero, his wife, Carmen, and their three children have arrived. All, the article reported, were wearing orange wrist bands for the next few weeks.

The lead article, with a large banner headline, was the expected imminent return of the Green Turtles and a very emotional discussion of whether electronically tracking them was an invasion of their privacy and sanctity. Did tiny transmitters interfere with navigation? Did attaching them to the shell irritate the wearer? Did sonar interfere with them? Were lights on desde Desdemona making it harder to find the beach?

*　　*　　*　　*

It is 2 am. Jeremy and Rosa run barefoot over the walkways. The only sounds are the patter of their feet on the boards and their heavy breathing. They stop at various houses gently to wake tourists. They knock, then say, "Please come now if you wish to see the turtles." Most of the locals have already assembled at the edge of the beach in the tree line. Many carry mangoes; some burn incense and ghee lamps; others softly chant, "Om Tara Tuttare Ture Svaha." Some carry yellowed pictures of Oscar. And some children have constructed of green fabric a large turtle shell that can be worn by 6 children as they dance and run across the beach.

At last a first green turtle emerges from the waves, and slowly begins its ascent up the beach. Everyone leaves the beach and moves further into the trees. All are silent. The turtle pulls hard with its flippers, and the shell gouges the sand. Its mouth is open as it breathes hard. Each push with its flippers is rewarded with only a few inches of forward progress and is impeded by a bow wave of gouged sand which will have to be climbed. Soon other turtles follow. They too struggle intently up the beach to dig holes with their flippers, to lay their hundreds of eggs, and to bury them in the sand.

Eventually, the turtles turn and push and slide and drag their way back to sea. They will not emerge for another year. The sea embraces and enfolds them. As soon as they reach the water, their full mobility is restored and they are swiftly gone. The male turtles remain behind in the sea, just beyond the shore, waiting patiently for their safe return.

When the last turtle has reached the sea, all of the people standing in the trees link arms and begin a snaking, chanting, joyful dance. The dance, originated by Milagros and Saraswati, is designed to prevent the sea birds and other predators from bothering the eggs until the tide returns to hide and cover them, and to thank the goddess for her preservation of peace and her teachings of compassion for the island. Drums emerge and torches. Bonfires soar. The dance lasts until the sun has risen. Then the entire island gathers for prayers of Thanksgiving on the beach before the altar built by Oscar and for a communal breakfast with mangoes, papayas, bananas, and pineapples and small sweet rolls shaped like turtles, each of which has a small square fleck of shiny, green nori seaweed on its top.

*   *   *   *

Oscar and Swamiji are sitting near the beach neck deep in water. They are watching the sun set across the water. Oscar explains how thankful he is that the dolphins took him to desde Desdemona and gave him a home when he and Milagros were adrift at sea, and he expresses his gratitude for the Goddess and the delight and peace that have been her grace on his every day on desde Desdemona. "When I die," he says, "I want to be floated into the sea so that our friends, the dolphins, may say goodby and push me gently and quietly away from desde Desdemona. Then my body can be a source of food for the birds and the big fishes." He smiles. "In fact," he says, "I hope that I die in my sleep while floating, that my dreams just subside in forgetting, and that I simply disappear. When I have left my body, and have completed my journey and become purely nonphysical, I want to return to desde Desdemona in dreams and thoughts to inspire the preservation of earthiness and simplicity here. That can be my legacy to my children and grandchildren. I will be a bringer of dreams."

Swamiji smiles. "Let us make an offering to Tara, to express out hope and prayer that it will be so. Let us hope you remember to have the name of the Goddess on your lips when you go, and that you leave the cage through the top of your head. That assures a good next birth." They stand, link arms, and walk toward the trees. There they pick two mangoes and place them on the altar.

CHAPTER 10

▼

It is 4 pm and raining. The rain is warm and the drops are heavy. They splatter on the roofs, and rain drips from the branches. The walkways are slippery. The wind occasionally gusts, pushing the rain through the open, glassless windows of the dwellings despite the deep overhangs of their roofs. Almost all of desde Desdemona seems to be wrapped in grey, warm wool and to be asleep. Ona and Bardo stand on the porch looking out to a grey and pink sea. The sea is freckled with driving rain.

"I have some amazing news," Ona says. Bardo understands immediately that this is to be a rare and important communication, one set off with a headline. He inhales. "When I was meditating this morning, my thoughts wandered to Oscar and Swamiji, how they came to venerate the Great Mother. And I thought about how the Mother appeared to them in dreams and visions and how she spoke and communicated. And about the mango offerings to her and the dance and the Thanksgiving festival. And about Milagros and Saraswati. I love to think about them. And how Tara told them that she would be present if called and that she'd reveal herself to others here. And while I was thinking about this, I became aware that there was something, a being quite nearby." At this she pauses and looks at him to see if he understands. He seems to be listening and returns her gaze; she continues. "I was surprised by this. That's never happened to me before. I was perfectly calm. So I wanted to understand what was happening, and I asked who it was."

At this point, Ona's throat tightens. Her voice is slightly squeezed. "She had a very deep, slow, rich voice. She said she was Tara, already well known to me, the Great Mother, on whose back we have made out home." She pauses to breathe audibly in and out. Her voice remains choked. "She is the goddess of action and protection and compassion. Of abundance and growth. The ancient one laden with eggs who ferries us from birth to death, from illusion to our enlightenment, across the sea of thoughts. And to my utter surprise and deep amazement, she said that I was now ready and that I can communicate with her whenever I wish to." Ona closes her eyes and begins to sob.

Bardo hugs her to him. Her tears roll onto his shoulders. "There's more," she says, lifting her eyes to look into his. "She says that she's been waiting for me to be ready for some time, and that she's pleased that the time has now come for me to flower and to set fruit and that I'm now able for her to come to me." She continues to cry.

"And there's more," she sobs. "It seems that I can make contact with her now at will, that I can make clear contact with her within seconds of requesting that she be in contact with me. I've done it three times since early this morning. I'm able to find her and connect with her whenever I try." She continues to sob and to hold him. "She is so huge, so full of grace and helpfulness."

The rain continues to splatter. In the distance a faint yellow line emerges at the horizon, the promise of a clear evening and a multitude of stars. Bardo is happy. Ona's readiness, her access to the unseen world, now at last strongly confirmed to her, is something he has known about and celebrated and appreciated for years and years. He is not surprised at all. He is pleased that she has at long last fully accepted this gift, a gift bequeathed to her long ago by Milagros.

*   *   *   *

Arjuna sits waist deep in the sea. He conducts a Socratic disputation with himself. Since his nocturnal visit to Swamiji, he has often amused himself by conducting outrageous dialogues with himself. These dialogues have been a gift to Arjuna of profoundly silly enjoyment, and for the others on desde Desdemona they have created delight in the space where there used to be the clamor of his arguments and his struggling toward awakening.

"But but but but but," Arjuna gestures, "You're leaving out something very important!"

"No, I'm not"

"Yes, you are"

"No no no"

"Yes yes yes. It is very very important. Ah hah! It is! I show you it is!"

At this he is convulsed in laughter. He rolls onto his side. The side of his head hits the sea. "Ooh! It's water. I'll drown."

"No you won't!"

"You silly man, you will. Now pay attention!"

Two pelicans are watching Arjuna from the beach.

"Go away you feathered elephants! We are discussing something of great societal and spiritual importance."

"Do not talk to birds like that! Respect them as sentient beings. They unlike you can fly."

"Cannot."

"I see. I suppose you can fly now! Amazing what a small hint, a tiny particle of enlightenment can accomplish is it not?"

At this the birds scramble toward the waves, Arjuna starts laughing and slapping the water with both hands, flapping his arms like wings. The splashes immediately propel water up his nose and down his windpipe.

He begins to cough and sputter. "Water in your nose again! In your lungs. Drowning!"

"Silly man, pay attention! Serves you right disturbing the noble birds."

He continues to slap the water and to laugh. His delight is complete. His absorption is thorough.

Saraswati stands on the deck and sees him splashing and howling with laughter. She remembers the arguing, worried, secretive man who arrived on desde Desdemona with her lugging his secret suitcase. The man who bit his nails. The one who frowned. She marvels that this practitioner of outrageous slapstick, of crazy kidding, is actually the very same person.

$$* \qquad * \qquad * \qquad *$$

Marley stands at that back of the classroom. The children smile at him; his relationship with Mari is both a confirmation of the ease of finding an off-island mate and a new romance to watch. Mari stands before the class. In the wake of the success of her previous short story, she was invited to compose another for the class. Today she is to read it.

"Once upon a time, a long way from here, I lived in a country with high mountains and the bluest of skies. The air was thin and the sun was extremely bright. I had the job of arising before the sun and taking the yaks to water and grass. They knew me and they trusted me to find for them fresh food and water every day. Sometimes we had to travel a long way to find these. Sometimes they were right at our feet. I spent my days with the yaks and only infrequently saw any people.

"One day, when it was quite sunny and the wildflowers hummed with bees, I sat with my feet in a stream. The water was icy and my feet turned blue and numb from the cold. And I wondered, "Where do all the streams go? Where do they end up?" The question wouldn't go away, so I began to ask everyone in my family and village about where all the streams went and where they all end up.

"My grandmother told me that all streams run down, that they get wider and wider as other streams join them, and that finally all the streams end up in an ocean. But she had never seen an ocean. Nor had anyone else in my village, nor had any of the traveling merchants who came to our village. Indeed, the lama in our village said that he had heard that the ocean had enormous fish in it, but that it was an extremely long journey to reach it, and that neither he nor anyone he knew had ever seen the ocean. But, he said, he believed that you could not see to the end of it, it was that big. And you could not walk all the way around it even in several life times.

"How could there be anything like that? I wondered. Even the tallest mountains have beginnings and ends. You can walk all the way around Mount Kailash. There is no mountain so wide that it cannot be circumambulated. I could not imagine what the ocean would look like. And how would I find the ocean if I wished to see it? That much seemed easy. I would find a stream and follow it down hill until its final end at the ocean.

"When I was 19 I decided to leave my home village and to walk to the ocean. I had been thinking about making this journey for four years. I took my robe and my alms bowl and I set out down stream. Each morning I asked for alms in whatever village I was in. If there were no village, I did not eat until I came to one and could beg for a meal. At night I slept in the open and saw the stars, or I slept in huts and houses where I was invited to rest. Each step I took I practiced mindfulness, each step I took I had gratitude that I could take yet another step and walk toward the ocean.

"After some time, my stream turned into a small river, and my river became wide, and many other rivers entered it. Each day I walked downstream. Each step I took was a step toward the ocean. After months of walking, there was a new smell in the wind. The smell was fresh and unlike anything I had experienced before. It seemed sharp and wet and sweet all at once. I inhaled it deeply and smiled.

"I had the idea that the wide river would soon end and that at its end would be the end of my journey. The anticipation of seeing the ocean made my heart pound in excitement. I walked over a knoll of white sand and there, in front of me, was the ocean. I walked straight ahead into it until the water reached my mouth. I was so happy that my tears mixed with the ocean. I looked across the ocean and could not see the other side, only the ocean and the sky. Later, I built a hut on the shore and I have lived next to the ocean ever since. I have gotten to know the ocean well.

"Lately, I have the idea that there might be lands in the ocean that I cannot see from here and that I will visit them also. I have no idea what these lands are like or who lives there and no one I have met is aware of them or where they might be. Even the fishermen here have not seen them. That will be my next journey. I will take it when the season calls for it."

All the children in the class applaud. Most think that she has written down the story of Swamiji's earliest travels. Travels before he sailed to desde Desdemona. They wonder how Mari could have learned Swamiji's story so soon. Did he tell it to her? They notice that they all know his story, but that he has never told it to them. Have their parents told this story to them? No. How then do they know this story? How can you remember something that you don't know?

✳   ✳   ✳   ✳

Ona and Carmen sit on the beach. "Manuel is happy fishing every day, he's enjoying feeding people ceviche and snappers, and he's begun working on his memoirs. He is writing down ideas in a notebook. He's become a fisherman and has stopped wearing the orange bracelet. He makes jokes with the other fishermen about St Paul. In fact, he's delighted that he has been unable to identify a single member of the oppressed underclass here and that the fishermen are all equals. He is looking for the hidden hand of globalization and imperialism, but hasn't quite located it yet. And me? I am ready for some work also. What I'm really interested in more than anything else at the moment is the history of desde Desdemona."

Ona is pleased. She loves the story of desde Desdemona, especially the arrival of Oscar and Milagros. "The oldest person born on this island is Oscar Sanchez, Jr. He was born here. He can tell you about our family, who were the original settlers. And he can tell you all about the role of the dolphins and the turtles and Saraswati and Arjuna. And, of course, you can talk with Swamiji. He might answer your questions. So far, the story is only oral. I don't think anybody's been writing it down. If you want any help at all, don't hesitate to ask."

Carmen looks puzzled. Ona sees that the dolphins and turtles part of the story is not exactly the dialectical materialism Carmen has been accustomed to, and that Carmen may be in for a big league surprise. Ona touches her on the hand, "It's even more fascinating than you might anticipate. Start with Oscar, Jr. Be sure to ask him about his birth." She smiles. Carmen smiles back.

Ona thinks about this story. She knows that some will not be able to believe it. Some will say it's just not true. Some won't accept it. But, she thinks, it doesn't really matter. There's more to this than the facts. Sometimes the truth isn't factual.

*   *   *   *

It is late Sunday afternoon and again Marley is limping. Every time he puts his foot down, his swollen ankle screams out. It is turning purple. And he's complaining. And he is using the cane with the carved toucan at the top. "It's like this. I used to push Ben around in front of the goal. But now he's back. He's stronger, and bigger, and faster, and unintimidated. And he always could run and dribble. So. He got around me for the third time today, and it was only Bardo in front of the goal. So I pulled him down by the shirt collar. He bounced off Ramirez and landed on my ankle. And Ramirez says I'm stupid because I should've fouled him outside the box when he first came to me. And he scored anyway after that only on the PK. I don't know why Bardo and Ona decided to send him off island to school. It's messing up the game."

Estrella's concern about Marley's pain and limping makes a slight crease in her forehead, but Ona's smiling anyway. "You need to take this injury to Lynette and see if she will treat it. And you better ask her very, very nicely indeed, because, as you know, Lynette is reluctant to treat any more Sunday game injuries. She thinks that her saving people like you from pain will make the game more violent, even more injurious. I think she got this idea from her grandmother. The dolphins never understood soccer at all. They don't have anything that separates their games from whatever else they do; their whole life is their game. Anyway, the grandmother got to the point when she was old where she wouldn't treat any more soccer injuries. Especially those in which John Coltrane Ramirez played even a small part. She would swim away or, if it was really painful, she would call Lynette's mom and see if she would be willing to heal it. Anyway, you may as well swim out there and call out for her. The herbs and things will take much, much longer. Mari will enjoy this, I think. I doubt she's ever seen anything like this before."

The crease in Estrella's forehead has become deeper. The corners of her mouth are tight. Something, she thinks, is quite peculiar here. Marley seems to have omitted something important from his descriptions of his life in desde Desdemona. In particular, that there is a very unorthodox health care system here. Are these people just putting me on?

Marley immediately notices her expression. He puts his non-cane arm around her shoulder, leans slightly on her, and says, "Well, I know this is a small surprise. This island has had a special relationship with the dolphins for more than this century. Swim out with me and watch what happens. You'll like it." Estrella bites her bottom lip, but she slowly walks with hobbled Marley to the shore, and swims off with him.

CHAPTER 11

▼

The rain bends the palm branches. It drips from every spiked leaf. The rain is heavy, but there is no wind. The air between the raindrops is saturated with mist. Small birds huddle close to the tree trunks and under eaves, ruffling their feathers and waiting. There are puddles on the walkways. The rain makes pocked patterns on the sea that shimmer and migrate like flocks of migrating birds. Ona and Rosa sit facing each other on a hammock, huddled over a battered wooden box, their legs crossed before them.

Rosa holds a faded, browned photograph of a strikingly beautiful, bare breasted woman standing on the beach, her arms on her hips, facing the camera. She is wearing a batik cloth about her hips and a radiant smile. "This," Ona says, "is the famous photograph of your great grandmother. Isn't she beautiful? I bet you don't remember her very clearly. But you used to sit on her lap, and she would tell you about the magical plants. And about how to use them. She didn't look like this then, did she."

Rosa shakes her head. "She looks like you, mama," she says, holding the photograph up next to Ona's face. "She looks like you." She stares from face to photograph and photograph to face. She touches Ona's cheek. She smiles. She puts the photograph gently back in the box. "There are other treasures, too," she says. She pulls from the box a heavy gold coin.

"And this," Ona says, "is a piece of Uncle Arjuna's great fortune. Would you like to tell me the story of how it got into Great Grandma's treasure box?"

Rosa shakes her head. She turns the coin over and over, looking at the stern face of distant, unnamed royalty on one side and then the winged angel on the other. She smells the coin. It is cool on her nose and shiny and slippery. She returns the coin to the box; her hand rummages and re-emerges with a small sand dollar, hanging from a piece of seaweed string. She holds the sand dollar out on her palm so that Ona can see it. "And this, this was left behind when Great Grandpa left his body. Tell me the story of it."

"I would rather listen to you tell it. Would you tell it for me?" Rosa shakes her head. She would rather hear it again.

*   *   *   *

"When Great Grandpa was very old and tired, he used to spend the afternoons sleeping in the sea or in the hammock over there in the trees. And in the late afternoons, after his nap, he would visit Swamiji. They were two old men, and they didn't say much then. They sat together without much talking. Sometimes they broke their silence and they laughed out loud about things. And sometimes you could here them chatting softly and laughing if you snuck up behind them. Swamiji would sometimes get interrupted by the disciples and have to tell his disciples things they should do. Then he and Grandpa would laugh about whatever the disciples wanted and whatever Swamiji had told them to do. One late, hot afternoon, Great Grandpa realized that he was finally ready to leave desde Desdemona and his body and to become a light being and return to being pure energy. He had been thinking about this, and had been talking with Swamiji about it, and had been praying to Mother Tara to guide his journey gently and safely from this world to the next. Up until then, he always wore the sand dollar around his neck. He said goodby to Swamiji, by placing his forehead against Swamiji's, and then he came home to his house over there. There, he gave Great Grandma the sand dollar. He put it around her neck. And he kissed her.

"She knew this meant that her husband was ready to leave his body and to enter the next world, and she knew how he wanted to do that. So she took his hand and walked slowly with him to the edge of the sea. As they walked so slowly down the beach, they began softly to chant the Tara prayer.

"When they reached the edge of the sea, Great Grandma cupped her hands together and called out to the sea, 'Friends, my beloved is ready, help him on his journey.' I imagine that her voice cracked, and that she shed a tear, but that then she called out a second time more strongly. Then Great Grandma gave Grandpa a big hug and a kiss and Great Grandpa got into the water, stretched out on his back, and began to float off toward the end of the reef. As he floated he hummed the Tara prayer, and he began to fall asleep. Great Grandma watched him until the dolphins joined him and surrounded him. That was how he left desde Desdemona and his body."

"But you left out the part about where the sand dollar came from in the first place and that's my favorite part."

*   *   *   *

"Your Great Grandfather gave Lisette lots and lots of dream images of the vast rain forests, the enormous Kapok trees, the vines, the ants weaving highways up the Acacia trees, the bats hanging in their small caves and crevices, his recollection of the wet, rich, delicious smell of the place, and the orchestra of sounds of insects and birds and howler monkeys bellowing. And Lisette kept these memories like precious jewels in her heart and shared them with the other dolphins.

"One day, Lisette, to thank your Great Grandfather for the exquisite gifts he had given to her and the other dolphins, brought him from far, far away, in a distant, colder, greyer ocean the small sand dollar shell. She and her pod had carried it for weeks and thousands of kilometers to bring it back to Grandpa. They wanted to give it to him to thank him for all the dream pictures he had given them.

"When they arrived with the sand dollar shell, your Great Grandpa was asleep in the sea, and he was dreaming about how the huge mother turtle feasted on sea weed. He was imagining the huge turtle's delight at discovering a delicious, new field of tender sea weed and her feelings of joy and gratitude for its great abundance, and he was enjoying her delight in each slow, tasty mouthful. The dolphins, of course, saw his dream, and they too began to enjoy the turtle's delight and appreciation. They decided to push Grandpa gently to shore without interrupting him.

"When his head touched the beach, Grandpa's mind shifted away from the turtle's feast. And he discovered in its place in his mind a message from Lisette. The dolphins, he understood, wanted to thank him and show their appreciation to him for all of the jewel-like dreams and pictures of the forest he had given them. He felt a welling up of joy and delight in his chest, his body became warm, and his eyes filled with tears of joy and thankfulness. You remember that tears are the oil that opens the rusty doors of the heart? And around his neck he found this sand dollar on a length of seaweed string. He recognized it as a special dolphin gift. He wore it from that day on until he left desde Desdemona. It was so precious to him that he regularly replaced the string just to keep it safe and secure."

*   *   *   *

The rain continues. Ona is alone. She stands before a large mirror. She holds the old photograph of Milagros next to her face toward the mirror, so that she can turn her gaze from the picture to her face and return to the picture. She is looking for the traces of Milagros in her face, the traces that Rosa has noticed.

Near her dark, sparkling eyes, in the bones of the forehead and cheeks she initially finds a resemblance. She also finds a similarity in the lines at the edges of her eyes when she smiles. And in the bridge of her nose. But the thought arises that the similarities are not solely in particular elements of Milagros's face, but in something deeper, something not quite entirely physical. Ona lets her focus become softer and fuzzier, and as she gazes from her face to Milagros and back, the nature of the strong similarity becomes more apparent and stronger. To be sure there is a blood connection and a blood resemblance between the two, but there is also a more profound connection of spirit, of a continuation of a lineage linking them. Ona notices it. She finds her grandmother's intense, bright light, and her communication with spirit on her own face. She backs away from the mirror, and she finds her grandmother's spirit hovering on her body. The births of Ona's three children and time and gravity have not erased her similarity with the younger Milagros in the photograph. Ona's memories of Milagros in old age, small, slightly bent, smiling, holding on the railing as she climbs the stairs, come flooding back to her. She recalls Milagros tending a plant. Milagros is kneeling and her arms are elbow deep in the soil. She is talking softly to the spirits and devas supporting the plant, offering them encouragement and praise. That is the Milagros Ona now sees alive in herself. The Milagros who talks with plants. The Milagros who has direct connection to Tara.

Ona feels deep love for her grandmother, and she misses her. She looks at herself in the mirror. "Ah Grandmother," she whispers, "What a treasure house you have given to me." She gazes at herself in the mirror. She notices that a vine has climbed up the back of the mirror and is reaching out for the light. She sees a bat hanging from the ceiling. Birds sing in the distance. The opulence of Milagros's gift is everywhere. And it is in everything.

*   *   *   *

Marley finds Mari on the deck. He can see that there is definitely trouble in Paradise. She is pacing and there is a tension in her shoulders that is driving them relentlessly toward her ears. Her hands are clenched tight in fists as hard as rocks. She has a bitter tear on her cheek, and her jaw is tightly clenched. He has no idea what's wrong.

"There's a problem," she says, as if he couldn't tell. "You know the laptop, the one I've been writing the novel about desde Desdemona in? Well, this morning, it wouldn't turn on. It's dead. The novel is in it and I can't get it out. I'm an idiot: I didn't back it up. It's almost 30,000 words, and I might have lost it all." She releases a high, shallow sigh from her chest. "Bardo says that he thinks the hard drive is ok, and that something else in the computer is what's wrong. He's taken it now to see if somebody off island can fix it. They'll know something in a few days or so."

Marley is speechless. The situation, he imagines, is worse than grim. Bardo knows how to get computers to work, he thinks, but this sounds awful. Mari continues to pace for a few minutes. Marley watches her in silence. His mind is racing through a Rolodex wheel of hackers, geeks, nerds, fixers, silently and desperately searching for the purveyor of technological miracles.

Mari, meanwhile, is in turmoil. "Is this what happens to me because of desde Desdemona? I'm helpless to get this fixed quickly. I can't go down the street and find a repair shop. Even in San Juan I could get this repaired today, or at the least know it would be all right. Is this the price of being here? There's a problem with time here."

Marley is silent. He knows the issue is not dependence or convenience. He's been at home in desde Desdemona long enough to know otherwise. The issue, he thinks, is never what one thinks it is. It's almost always something else. Things, as Bardo always reminds him, are not what they appear to be, nor are they otherwise. When things are like this, impermanence is an ally. Everything is always changing. Sometimes too slowly. He waits for a change to arrive.

At last Mari asks herself aloud. "What's the point of this, why am I seeing this?" Marley senses that relief has almost arrived.

"There must be a reason, something I need to know that the computer crash is trying to tell me." She continues to pace, and the tightness is only slightly abated. "I wonder, I wonder," she thinks as her brain scans everything without making a connection and as she tries to get her breath down past her sternum. She looks out at the sea and the reef. The sun glints on the water and there are big, tall billowing clouds at the horizon that might turn to lightning and rain. Finally, she manages to inhale deeply as she paces. Marley continues to hope and watch and wait. His mental Rolodex has come up only with mirages and hallucinations of unknown, bearded slide rule types with pocket protectors and Japanese accents who are inaccessible and mysterious, but he knows that the answer is not in there. It's not the computer, he thinks.

A thought is organizing and slowly unfolding itself in Mari. "I am having fear and discomfort about the computer crash and my novel because I believe something that is incorrect. I guess I am afraid because I believe that there is only a short supply of creativity for me. If my hard drive has a convulsion and loses my novel, I believe I will not be able to recreate it or create another that is as good or, for that matter, ever find another, better one. I'm holding onto scarcity, and I'm holding on to it with a clenched fist.

"I'm seeing this this way because I am believing something about myself that's wrong. It's a belief I can change. The mistake is focusing on scarcity and lack and grasping after the missing productivity. The fact is that the stream of creativity is infinite, and that there is no drought, no scarcity of it for me. It's not a matter of my faith in something I ought to believe. It's about whether I fully appreciate the extent of the flow of creativity and abundance and am willing to continue fully to connect with it.

"I have needed to discover this information. I know everything is all right. I hope I didn't lose the whole book." She begins to have a very slight smile at the edge of her lips. Marley's relief at this is palpable. His mind still searches for someone who through brilliance or dumb luck can fix the unfixable, but the search has been transformed by the smile to one for subsidiary insurance rather than for adept crisis intervention.

"It's scary," she says at last. "But I think everything is going to be all right. If I weren't here in desde Desdemona, I wouldn't have understood this." Marley is sure that he, too, hopes that everything is going to be all right.

*   *   *   *

Rosa has a hand and finger play. She makes a fist. On each of her four fingers is a letter, so that her closed fist says "THIS." "THIS" she says "IS" Jane. She opens her hand. On her palm is a picture of a girl with a smile on her face. She closes her fist. "Jane (showing her palm) says "HI," she says. Then she says, "THIS" "IS" Jane, again showing the palm. She claps her hands together, "when the train goes by." On her right hand is a picture of smashed up Jane. Rosa squeals and laughs.

Mari wonders what name she could give to the computer hard drive. Maybe it could be Jane. She wonders what kind of runaway train she has conjured up when, she imagines, a soft, sweet whisper from a hummingbird would have sufficed.

*   *   *   *

Bardo is soaking wet and carrying a large package. He is wearing a yellow rain suit with yellow rain pants. He is wearing a baseball hat with "Industriales" on it. He hurries up the steps and stands, wringing wet, before Mari. Only the slight twinkle in his eyes gives him away. From his pocket he produces one compact disc. "Here," he says, handing it to Mari. "One incipient novel. Dr. Frankenstein had to do a, shall we call it an autopsy, on your laptop to preserve this small segment of its brain. Your laptop, I regret to inform, simply is no more. He reduced it to its lowest common denominator. He, of course, backed this up before giving me the cd so that he could clone another one if ever required to do so by the forces of good or evil mischief. Under the circumstances, I felt compelled to bring you something to celebrate with." In the package is a brand new state of the art notebook, a carton full of cds, and two ripe, yellow mangoes.

CHAPTER 12

▼

Swamiji is lying at the edge of the sea. He has made a pile of sand to rest his head upon. He lets his feet and lower body float in the surf. His hair is completely grey and full of sand. His browned belly is a small, rounded hillock. He is quite old. He estimates his age as 95 years. His disciples say he does not look at all like a 95 year old, but none of them is sure if they've ever seen anybody else that old. He seems to be quite flexible and vigorous. Leaning over him is one of his disciples. Swamiji, who is not wearing sunglasses, directs the disciple, waving his one hand back and forth while the other screens the sun from his eyes. "You have to move this way. No. Too much. Back a little. Are you watching? Is your shadow in my eyes? Good. Now I can see you." He starts to laugh.

"Sri Swamiji," the disciple begins. Swamiji notices the "Sri" and is instantly sure that the question about to be raised concerns the much ballyhooed issue of his eventual demise, the transmission of his lineage, and power in the ashram. "I take it this is about life and death?" Swamiji interrupts. "More particularly, my life and death. That Sri always gives you all away. When it's about food, drink, sex, and squabbles in our community, you never ever bother to use that. Sri is reserved to announce arguably serious topics, and particularly when I will be leaving my body. Sri and my mahasamadhi are inseparable from each other." He laughs. His belly rocks side to side. "Am I mistaken?"

"Swamiji," the disciple begins again. His face is tighter, and his jaw is set against the near certainty that Swamiji will derail his inquiry and suggest some sort of dietary regimen to bring clarity to the disciple's mind via his stomach. He is careful to keep his shadow across Swamiji's eyes. "I want to ask you about who will be in charge when you have your mahasamadhi. Who will you place in charge?"

"This is a most unsurprising question. It is not interesting because it does not focus on the present, on appreciation of the present, and complete immersion in and enjoyment of the grace of the present. It is, unfortunately, a disconcertingly perpetual question. I take it that you and my other disciples have decided that I might go sooner, rather than later?" He starts to giggle. "That is most humorous. Who can know when it is time to go? Why just now, I was thinking about my dear departed friend, Oscar. Now that man knew when it was time to go! And he left exactly when it was time. But he certainly did not have it decided for him by a committee, did he?" Swamiji is smiling. "Move this way, please, you have to watch where your shadow goes. And who did Oscar leave in charge?" At this the smile turns into gales of giggles.

"Anyway," Swamiji says when he recovers from the giggling, "I have decided to hang around for the foreseeable future. There is no reason I am aware of why I cannot live to 103 years old. So I have a little time left. Please go tell your friends who are interested in this topic that I will go 11 days after my 103rd birthday. Also, tell them that if they continue to ask, I may change my plans and stay for longer or shorter. Oh. Eat nothing but lemon water and grapes for a while." At this Swamiji laughs, closes his eyes, and begins to hum a song. It sounds a lot like a Hindustani version of Bob Marley's "No Woman, No Cry."

Soon he feels tapping on his shoulder. "Those disciples," he thinks, noting their insistence and insatiability. Opening one eye, Swamiji looks directly into Rosa's' face. "Swamiji," she says "I want to ask you a question. May I?"

"Oh I love it when people are polite. I can tell that they are not my disciples." He starts to laugh. "Of course you may ask. I do hope I have an answer. If I don't know the answer, can I make one up?"

"Swamiji, do you know where the statue of Tara came from, the one that is in Great Grandpa's altar? I would like to know."

"That is something I cannot answer, my little one. However, if you lean over, I will give you my blessing on your head. Then you may ask your mother, who now knows better than anyone around here, about all things concerning Tara."

Rosa kneels down, and Swamiji touches her on her forehead with his thumb. It feels slightly fizzy to Rosa. She thanks Swamiji and wanders in search of Ona.

*   *   *   *

Bardo is stretched out in the hammock. He is doing an exercise Swamiji told him about. He gets completely comfortable and relaxed. Then he thinks of something about which he has only positive thoughts. At the moment, he is thinking about how delicious it feels when he is in good physical condition and is running in the New York Marathon. He focuses on his enjoyment, his appreciation of the event, his excitement, the ease of it. As he thinks of these things, other positive thoughts come to him as well, thoughts about how his body is healthy, strong, light, swift, lithe, thoughts about how wonderful and efficient his breathing feels. Soon his mind has appreciated the running, and moves to appreciate something else. He continues as long as there is purely positive thought. At the first awareness of a negative thought he stops, pauses, and returns to the beginning again. Bardo is agog at how many negative thoughts arise in his thinking. Some, he notes are obviously comparative, critical, negative; others, implicitly negative; others, disguised as neutral are negative. He goes back to running down Fourth Avenue in Brooklyn in a sea of runners, enjoying the spectacle of it all, cradled in positive thought, and falls asleep with his mouth open and his jaw hanging relaxed.

*   *   *   *

Milagros and Oscar are cleaning a huge fish on the beach for a dinner for Swamiji's disciples. These dinners, attended by the entire community, occur every few weeks now, whenever Oscar has caught a tremendous fish. Arjuna arrives. "Have you ever seen such a beautiful fish?" he asks himself aloud. "I am sure that this wonderful fish is for some special event," he tells Milagros. "I know that because it is cooperating with you and not resisting." He starts to laugh. "Can you imagine what this task would be like if our friend here, the guest of honor, changed its mind and decided to walk away? All its effort would have to go into growing legs and pushing you away from it instead of its present serenity." Arjuna continues to talk to himself as he wanders off down the beach. "It is because he has surrendered himself," he whispers. "It is because he understands what comes after the seeming end and is ready now for that adventure to begin. He graces and nourishes our community as his final physical act. Soon he will be pure spirit again. May I have such a useful exit."

*   *   *   *

Bardo's dream of running has begun to take a weird turn. The streets have begun to shake and the buildings have begun to vibrate menacingly. In his dream, he thinks, "New York doesn't have earthquakes, does it?" He tries repeatedly to ask the runners near him, "New York doesn't have quakes, does it?" but they don't respond. The rumbling drowns out his voice. Even he cannot hear his spoken words. They cannot hear him over the rumbling. The sound becomes even more intense. Bardo wakes up with a start and turns toward it. Over the sea, coming directly towards him he sees it. It is an old, huge propeller airplane, flying very close to the sea, flying directly at desde Desdemona. The airplane is green and brown, and it has four propellers. It is twisting from side to side, from wingtip to wingtip, as it flies, and its deafening noise shakes the tree houses. Bardo jumps out of the hammock, and throws himself on the deck. The airplane continues to rumble and twist toward the island. Bardo thinks that it will fly directly into the trees and the houses in desde Desdemona. He feels a scream rise in his chest and leave his mouth, but it too is drowned out by the engines of the airplane. He is lying on the vibrating deck. He wonders where Ona and the children are. At the last possible second, the airplane pulls up ever so slightly, and barely lumbers over the island, shaking it vigorously, breaking glass, driving people to throw themselves on the ground, sweeping dishes and books from shelves, narrowly avoiding a collision.

Bardo stands. Sweat covers his still vibrating body. He watches the plane as it continues to roar and twist north toward the horizon. He exhales deeply and notices how shaky he is, how unsteady the still rocking tree house is. The island trembles. The plane continues to grumble and twist until, out at sea, the tip of one of its wings scrapes the water. At that the plane begins to flip, groan, and cartwheel into a sudden eruption and shower of steel that scatters airplane components and flame and cargo. The engines and the bulk of the fuselage disappear below the surface, but the surface of the sea is strewn with a zillion pieces of airplane and tons of its cargo. The airplane has left an atoll of junk floating on the surface. The sudden silence stuns. Even the birds and insects have been shocked speechless. Bardo is without words. He runs with the rest of desde Desdemona to the beach. As he runs he hears children and adults crying and screaming and sobbing in horror and relief.

*   *   *   *

The first boat to reach the wreckage plows through a cold marijuana and salt water bisque with airplane parts and cargo croutons. The fires have extinguished, and the heaviest parts of the plane have sunk. The turquoise sea is littered with cakes of marijuana, crates of white powder, buoyant airplane components, and wood from packing crates. Dried and wet leaves and plastic packages of white powder float everywhere mingling with airplane, and their smell is astonishingly piquant and strong.

The boat drives in circles through the soup, looking for occupants of the plane. Acero is in the bow of the boat. "Fucking narcotraficantes," he mutters. "Don't give a fuck about anything but themselves. They tried to set up in San Sebastian, would have given us tons of money to help them launder their money, but they are ruthless, and deadly. Look at all of this coke and weed. The gringos are some consumers! What a taste they have for this shit. What assholes!" He interrupts himself to point and shout, "Over there, over there, what is that?"

The boat swerves around a chunk of plastic wrapping material toward a large box labeled "fragile, glass." Pushing up against the box and holding it steady above the water is a single dolphin, who squeaks when the boat arrives and then dives deep. On top of the box is a stunned, semi-conscious, thoroughly wet man wearing a leather jacket and a gaudy Rolex watch. He is a half drowned rat. He has a pointy nose and stringy, long hair. He lies on his back, his eyes closed. He has a gash in his forehead, and blood flows freely down his face. Standing on the man's arm is a grey parrot. Its feathers are rumpled, and it is squawking and screaming.

Acero and Marley pull the man gently into the boat. The parrot stops screaming and sits on a seat. The man opens his eyes slightly and, squinting out of swollen lids, feebly pulls a pistol out of his pocket. Water runs out of its unsteady, quivering barrel. Marley unceremoniously kicks it out of his hand. The gun flies overboard and sinks in the sea. In his best Humphrey Bogart voice Marley sneers, "You won't be needing that where you're going, Shweetheart." Acero frowns, "There are good reasons including that gun to drop him in the sea now and leave him here to drown. There are excellent reasons for making believe we did not find him and that the plane didn't crash here."

They continue to look for survivors for the next half hour. They find no one. As the boat turns for desde Desdemona, Acero says aloud what is on others' minds, "I really think we'd be a lot better off without this guy." At this the parrot responds, "Better off, Better off."

*   *   *   *

Ona has cleaned the man's wound and examined him. There is nothing wrong with him that she cannot heal given time. She gives him a special poultice of herbs for his head, and tells him to drink lots of water. She does not detect a concussion. She asks him his name. He responds, "I am in big trouble. I lost the plane. The cargo is a big deal, and the plane is an extremely big deal. It was a big plane." She asks again what his name is. He refuses to say. "Was there any one else on the plane when it crashed?" He shakes his head no. "Well," she says, "I have to call you something, so you get to pick a name." He looks at her incredulously, "You're not going to jail me or extradite me?" She laughs. "Some think we should have left you in the sea. But to where would I extradite you? And there's no jail here. You made a tremendous mess in the ocean, and you frightened us all deeply. But you committed no crime here. Anyway, what is to happen to you is a decision for the entire community here." A faint smile comes to his lips. He rolls over and falls sound asleep. Ona recalls that this is not the first fugitive from justice to land by surprise on desde Desdemona. She looks at the parrot. "Como se lllama?" she asks him. "Perdido," he squawks. "Perdido, perdido, perdido." Ona smiles at the idea of calling the parrot "Bird" and his master "Dizzy."

CHAPTER 13

▼

Precisely how Arjuna got his promotion to office work was unknown to them, but it was the subject of persistent rumors and gossip among his fellow railroad workers. Theirs was exhausting work, and their envy for the man who had left it behind without dying on the job was without limits. You could hear the rumors while they leaned on their shovels and picks. "He's been giving kick backs to the boss." "He's having relations with the foreman's wife." "He is a cousin of the straw boss." None of these made any sense. But in the heat of the jungle and during the long hours of back breaking work, the idea that one of their fellows had escaped their torture was unfathomable and an excellent and fully entertaining distraction.

The truth was actually much simpler. Like them, Arjuna despised the work, and he realized that he would never be able to stop working if things didn't change. But unlike them, he realized that if he spent time agonizing about it, either on or off the job, he would be even further mired in unhappy, angry, frustrated thoughts. Arjuna decided not to think about his work at all. Instead, he would spend his waking hours fantasizing and dreaming. And his favorite dream was of himself sitting in a white, starched shirt at the tall desk in the paymaster's office, surrounded by money, calculating workers' pay, filling in the books and ledgers, drinking ice water, occasionally pausing to read poetry, and enjoying the contrast of his white, laundered clean shirt with the muggy, sweaty, wilting, humid world surrounding him.

The images of himself as paymaster were so enjoyable, so fulfilling, such an engrossing pleasure, that he began in a way to enjoy the hours digging and lifting and moving the rails, when he could fully immerse himself in the paymaster's office of his mind, its water cooler, its slow fan on the ceiling, its shaded windows, the little green visor, the sleeves of his shirt folded up toward his elbows, and the pens and ink, the lined ledger paper, the smell of the dry wood floors, the sounds of insects during the siesta. Arjuna was so fully in the paymaster's office in his mind, and paying so little attention to the "reality" of his situation, that it came to him as no surprise whatsoever when the railroad's assistant paymaster died of the fever and he was told that he had been selected to become assistant paymaster.

Arjuna received the news at 5 p.m. on Tuesday and was required to report early the next morning. He spent all the money he then had on hand for a white shirt and other appropriate assistant paymaster accoutrements including a haircut and shave. When he arrived at the paymaster's office to begin work, he was every inch an archetypal assistant paymaster, but with two possible exceptions: his hands were extremely rough and callused from the months of rail work, and his haircut revealed that his tan did not quite touch the new line at which his hair met his forehead. These he noticed instantly and with pleasure. To himself in the mirror he said, "So there still is something more to be learned before I fit perfectly into my new job."

What Arjuna learned in the first weeks of his new job, was that the railroad was terribly and ineffectually managed. The accounts were a mess, the chief paymaster was drunk most days when he showed up, but he was absent more than he was present. No one had any idea how much money the railroad had, and to Arjuna's utter amazement, no one seemed to care. There had never been an audit. The owners, who were apparently somewhere in England, had never visited the island. He couldn't find any evidence that financial reports were ever sent to the owners.

One evening he returned home to Saraswati smiling. "Soon," he whispered, "Very soon, we are going to get out of here. We are going to go to Trinidad. We are going to be filthy rich, and I am going to concentrate on finding a great teacher." Saraswati nodded and went back to making papadums. She nodded to herself as well, "Arjuna got himself promoted. God knows how. Maybe he can move us away from here as well." The idea of being in Trinidad, away from the railroad and the railroad workers, away from this company town, the idea of being rich, the idea that she and Arjuna might find some kind of fulfillment, these ideas were enough to make her dizzy.

As she felt herself buzz from these thoughts, she slightly burned her little finger on the griddle. Shaking it in pain, and putting it in her mouth, she realized that she didn't know whether it was possible. The pain of the burn mirrored and amplified the pain of her doubt. Meanwhile, Arjuna was in the back room of the shack putting the first hand full of gold coins in the big suitcase under their bed.

*   *   *   *

Bardo and Marley are sitting in the sea in the office. "The flying Colombian," Bardo frowns. "It's remarkable that the crash only hurt his feelings. He's a pain in the neck, but he's quite healthy. He spends his days smoking weed, getting paranoid, and acting sketchy. I don't think he's going to fit in here at all. But I don't think anybody's going to come looking for him.

"He was flying low like that to avoid radar, so it's unlikely that his employers know where he went down. I don't think they can come looking for him or his cargo because he apparently wasn't following any pre-set course. If they do come, they're going to be armed and furious. The DC-6 was expensive, and it was carrying an awful large quantity of coke and weed. Where was he taking it?"

Marley shrugs. "He's not talking. He won't give his name. He won't say where he was going. We all assume he was flying from Colombia but it could have been from Venezuela or Guyana or someplace else. Frankly, I think he's afraid that somebody will find out where he is. Or that we'll turn him over to the US narcs, who will put him in prison for decades, or, worse for him, will let his employers know where he is."

Bardo stands up. "I'm going fishing with Acero." His shirt is soaking from mid-chest down, and his Industriales hat, which he plunges repeatedly in the sea and puts wet on his head, drips water down his face.

*   *   *   *

Saraswati didn't bring up the subject of being rich in Trinidad for the next three months, and she and Arjuna, as if by mutual agreement, never mentioned it again to each other. She noticed that Arjuna was slowly filling the suitcase, but she paid no real attention to its contents. Then, one evening, Arjuna came home smiling. Grinning and rubbing his hands together, he whispered, "Are you ready to leave now?"

"You mean now?"

"Can you be ready to leave later this evening?"

"What do I need to bring?"

"We need lots of water and food and blankets and knives and fishing equipment and this suitcase and hats, and I haven't got the slightest idea. You are supposed to have taken care of all of that by now. We're making a sea voyage to Trinidad. Have you really done nothing to get ready?"

"I can get ready now."

Arjuna was incredulous and impatient and astonished. "Didn't I tell you that we were going to Trinidad and to get ready for us to go?"

"You didn't tell me to get ready."

"How did you think we would get there?"

"I don't know. I will get ready now. I'll do it immediately."

"No," he shouted. "No. You have to be ready already. Not later. Now. It's a big thing. It is a sea voyage. Just the two of us. You have to have gotten everything ready long before now. We are going tomorrow. Now please get us ready." He is pacing back and forth, fuming. His words are staccato hisses as he restrains himself from further yelling. "Don't you understand? I have the money. I have a map. I have a boat at the dock. I did my part of this. What on earth have you been doing these past three months while I was doing my part of getting us ready?"

Saraswati is shocked. Is he really ready to leave? How can he be ready now? Is this some kind of delusion that has seized him? She can see that Arjuna is distraught that she has done nothing to prepare for the voyage. "No," she says with determination. "Not tomorrow. We will leave tonight anyway. Go outside and wait for me. I can get it all in the next hour or two, and when I have it, we will go tonight."

As she assembles their few most important possessions and the provisions she imagines they will need for several days at sea, Saraswati hopes that the rest of Arjuna's plans are more complete than his description to her of his plan for emigrating from the island. This thought, this fear feels like a small, hard cashew in her solar plexus or a pebble wedged in the arch of her foot.

*   *   *   *

The anonymous pilot stands on the beach watching Sunday soccer. He smells of weed. His eyes are red and glassy. He has not revealed his identity or anything else of importance since his arrival. Ona has pronounced him fit; Bardo and Marley, who wonder what the community will ultimately decide to do with him, do not feel any reason to encourage a swift decision.

Running back and forth on the sideline, Rosa and the younger Acero children have their own game. They come behind the goal when the ball is at the far half of the field and discuss the game with John Coltrane Ramirez. "Be alert," they shout to him. "It's coming this way. I hope you can stop it."

"I can, I can," he shouts back to them.

"You sure? You sure you can stop it?"

"Absolutely, absolutely sure. Nobody scores on me. Look at your dad," he says to Rosa, "Can anyone get past him to me? No. Not a chance."

"My dad is not nearly as fast as Ben," she says shaking her head. "He's old. He's even getting round in the belly."

Ramirez laughs. It's true. "It doesn't matter my little one," he says. "Your dad will hold tight onto his shirt. He'll never let him get past." At that Rosa and Ramirez both laugh; Bardo, who has overheard all of this, shouts at them, "There is much more to it than holding his shirt. There is also the matter of finesse. And experience. Not to mention skill. I've been doing this for years, you remember."

"I know, my friend, I know. For years and years. You don't have to remind me," Ramirez smiles.

The pilot, who stands next to Rosa, smiles at the remark. "How old are you?" he asks her.

"Eight."

"I thought so," he says. At this, his jaw quivers, and a small tear glistens in the corner of his eye. Noticing the tear, she wonders if he has a child her age. She wonders if the child knows that her daddy is far away but safe. To his surprise, she touches the back of his hand and says, "Kids love it here." Her hand is warm. Then she runs off with the pack.

*　　　*　　　*　　　*

After his dream of mother Tara, Arjuna sought out Oscar and Milagros. He found them tending their banana plants. "I want to thank you both," he told them. "You gave me everything I ever wanted. My life here has been wonderful."

Milagros stood. Her hands were black from compost. She smiled. "I think you wrecked your ship here, and that we gave you and Saraswati shelter. After that, whatever has happened is because of your clear desires and your intentions."

Arjuna nods. Then, his eyes squinting slightly, he clears his throat and continues, "Did you know that I brought a suitcase full of money when I arrived?"

"I know that you spent a lot of money when we have gone to other islands," Oscar says. "But it was none of my business. We have all benefitted from your labor and wealth and from your presence here and from your generosity."

"I have decided that it is not proper for me to keep this money, and I no longer want this money as a personal resource. Saraswati agrees with me about this. Instead, I have decided that all of the people on desde Desdemona should have what remains of this money that I brought with me. It is still quite a lot of money. And I want you, Milagros, by yourself, to take this one heavy, gold coin, with the angel on it, because you and Saraswati brought Swamiji to me, to us." He hands her the coin. She looks at it carefully.

"Why," she asks, "is it not proper for you to have this money? I don't understand."

"I am delighted," Arjuna replies, "that you asked me this. I will answer your question fully, but first you must promise me that you will nevertheless, no matter what I tell you, accept this coin as a token of my gratitude." He again places the heavy coin in Milagros' hand; it glistens atop the dark, moist compost. Milagros can feel both its surprising weight and how tightly it has been held in Arjuna's hand.

CHAPTER 14

▼

Rocking on the sea and sitting silently beside other quiet men slowly relaxed and soothed Manuel Acero. It became instantly familiar to him. It reminded him of being a small boy San Sebastian and fishing with his grandfather. Together they took the dugout and tied it to a pole embedded deep into the bottom of the river. Then, moored against the tide, they cast their lines—no poles were used—over and over and over again, catching the bounty of bass and bream the river brought to their bait. Mostly, they were silent. Sometimes Papa spoke to him. He recalled vividly Papa's slow, deep voice and the patience of his answers to life's questions. It was Papa who was the first to tell him that simple things, like catching a bass, were intended to be more delightful than castles and gold. Could a God who loved people reserve his most precious bounty for only the few? Of course not. Those who thought so didn't understand God. Then he'd smile, cast his line, and fall silent again.

As he sat on the smooth sea, line in hand, occasionally talking with his fisher-men companions, Acero's mind also wandered to the things that had brought him pleasure, and he enjoyed recalling the passion he felt about his movement. He thought about sugar cane. The lines of trucks, sitting in the sun, silent, brimming with cane, waiting for the factory. The knots of drivers talking, drinking, sleeping in their trucks. The brown canes piled high, baking in the sun. The hot trucks. The smoke of the factory billowing black against a blue sky. The drivers talking about love and politics. It was delicious to him, and just, that maximizing the profits of the factory created the queue of trucks, the waiting queue in turn created a forum among the many drivers for his revolution. The revolution, he sighed, it really was grown directly from the excess profits of the foreigners. He recalled strolling among the waiting trucks in the sun, talking, shaking hands, patting backs, mostly listening. "My brother," he would say. He knew these men. Sometimes he pointed at the electric wires running to the factory and wondered out loud what it would take to get the drivers electricity, and light, and refrigeration in their homes. What would it take to bring ice water? What would it take to bring the sounds of a radio?

On the smooth sea, the joyful, pleasurable memories were abundant. If pressed, he would have admitted his gnawing worries about how it would all turn out, and about Che and Grenada and Panama and Haiti, and about building a revolution that would bring joy to his island. But on the smooth sea, he was not pressed. His revolution to him was delicious, like lobster and conch kabob. And his marriage and children were the spicy habanero pepper sauce that made it fragrant and piquant. He smiled. He was truly thankful. How amazing that he should find himself in such luxury and peace.

∗   ∗   ∗   ∗

Knowledge of the plants was to be passed from generation to generation. Milagros began to learn of their qualities in her infancy. Her mother and her grandmother had both achieved the status of "snake doctor" and they consistently made available to Milagros all that they knew. This knowledge was not transmitted by lecture nor was it written down. Instead, in stories, demonstrations, and answers to questions they held nothing back. The knowledge, it was believed, could be revealed in all its magnificence solely when it was sought by the student. It was acknowledged that the knowledge was so very valuable that it could be discussed only when it was directly asked for. When Milagros plied her mother and grandmother with questions they were delighted. When she asked to watch them heal others, they brought her along while they healed wounds, sutured them with special ants, cured infections with poultices and teas, and answered the myriad requests for healing. Milagros stood at their side; before acting themselves, they always asked her what she thought should be done.

Although it was often repeated that there was no magic, that there was an explanation for everything, the results seemed to defy all logical explanations. How could a child's asthma be cured by special prayers, cutting a notch over her head on a particular kind of tree, and requiring her to walk out of the forest without turning back? If she never approached the tree again, even if she entered the same forest, her breathing would remain clear. Why was that? Surely, healing an upset stomach by chewing jackass bitters was different from this cure. Was it the particular prayer that was said? Was it not magic? Her mother would smile and pat her head. "There's no magic," she said. "Nothing we do is magic. I tell you this often, so you will remember. There is more to the world than you can see with your eyes. Much more. To enhance the body's natural healing, you have to sense the world very deeply, very completely. Your feelings are the map of how the world is. They are your guide. Your feelings are more precise and reliable in healing than your eyes or your thoughts will ever be."

Sometimes people arrived in the middle of the night when they were bitten by a viper. The venom broke down the blood, and it spouted from their wounds. When his happened, Milagros stood and watched while her grandmother stopped the bleeding and began the cure. These cures she memorized; they would keep the life from flowing away from the bitten person.

By the time Milagros and Oscar fled, Milagros's love of the plants and her knowledge of their powers had become complete. There was nothing that had not been transmitted to her and retained. Milagros had become a living repository of the knowledge, a powerful healer.

*   *   *   *

The pilot remained at the fringes of desde Desdemona for more than two weeks. He drank Havana Club rum straight from the bottle, and he smoked joint after joint. He did not share his intoxicants. Ona had ultimately pronounced him healed, but out of understandable paranoia, the fear that he would be jailed or deported or something worse, he remained in the shadows. Eventually, he left the shadows long enough to swim often in the sea, but he tried studiously to avoid Bardo and Marley out of fear that they would again confront him about who he was and what he was doing. It did not happen the way the pilot dreaded.

One morning the pilot was floating near the reef, snorkeling, watching the abundant sea life. He was particularly interested in a neon blue king parrot fish who was nibbling at the coral, munching his way at the deep fringe of the reef. The fish let him approach, but kept him at a distance of two meters. The pilot followed him, absorbed in the brightness of the coral, the rich color of the fish, the feeling of the sun on his back and neck, the rhythmic sound of his breathing through the snorkel. He did not know the date, or the time. Some water seeped into his mask, and he lifted his head out of the water to empty the mask and reseal it. As he tilted his mask back, letting the water out, he realized that he was only a few feet from an anchored fishing boat. In the boat he saw three or four men, including a man he had seen numerous times on television. The pilot stood on the reef.

"Are you Acero?" he asked.

"I used to be him. Now I'm somebody else. Are you a Colombian narcotraficante who used to fly a DC-6 and is now standing on the reef?"

"I used to be one. Now I have no name. I am disappeared."

"Well, don't stand on the reef. It kills it. You can come into the boat and we'll ask you about who you used to be and what you're being now."

It seemed to the pilot, who had been companionless and conversationless for quite some time, to be a reasonable enough, friendly enough request. He pulled himself over the gunwale and stood wringing wet in the boat. "You've already met Marley, haven't you?" Acero said pointing. "And today we have as a guest fisherman Bardo. Usually he doesn't come out here with me, but today he is here because he wants to pursue a possibly frustrating conversation with Marley about what to do about you and what the options are."

"About me?" the pilot asked. "Just don't tell anybody where I am, and don't put me in jail, and don't send me to the US. Anything else will be just fine with me."

Bardo laughed. "I suppose we should just give you a ticket for littering and messing up the sea. Or for illegally and unsafely parking an aircraft. Or for bad manners. Or failing to express gratitude for being plucked from the sea. Or for endangering the welfare of a bird."

Marley found this amusing. "The point he's trying to make is that you're not the first person who arrived here with a legal issue or two. But we've got a rule here, and that is that you can't stay unless you ask us to stay, and even then everybody has to agree that it's ok for you to stay. If you don't make a request to stay in the very near future, we have to get you off desde Desdemona, drop you off somewhere else. Perhaps Barbados or Antigua or someplace else you might pick."

The pilot was silent. It had never occurred to him that by crashing the aircraft he could end up in an extremely comfortable, very safe place. He realized that the tension in his upper back caused by the likelihood of deportation and long term incarceration was easing slightly. His breath deepened. But then there remained an intense ache in his chest. What about his family in Colombia? Would they be killed when he did not return? Would they be kidnaped and held hostage until he ransomed them? Would all of his possessions be taken and his family left without support? He was safe, but what of them? Wasn't he in some way flying partially for them too?

Bardo watched the relief spread across the pilot's face, and saw the new sadness almost immediately emerge. The pilot's mouth twitched slightly and contorted. He swallowed deeply, trying to gulp the sadness away. His eyes became moist and they darted side to side, from spot to spot. And a frown surfaced on his face. Acero saw it too.

"My friend," he said. "I came here, and I make my home here because my island was destroyed by a volcano. I was lucky. I could bring my family. I came here, if I can be blunt, because nobody else would have me. Not even Fidel. Can you believe that? It seems that you can be here also, if you want to be, because these people will probably allow you to stay. I will go along with the consensus, too, but in truth I must tell you that I despise narcotrafficking and those who ruin lives with it. Those like you. So if there is a reason why you cannot stay here, that will satisfy me a great deal. But you also need to know that this is the most compassionate island I have ever heard of, and that these people will not dwell in the past and they will help you to the extent they can. But they will not do a single solitary thing unless and until you ask them for their help." Acero looked out toward the sea and reeled his line slightly. There was no fish on it. Then he focused on the horizon.

Marley cast his line. Bardo looked at the pilot's face; the pilot stared back. The boat was silent, except for the clicking sound of Marley's star drag while he reeled in the slack. The pilot was the first to avert his eyes.

*   *   *   *

Rosa and Jeremy stand in waist deep, turquoise water. They are watching mangrove swallows harvest insects off the ocean. The swallows are skilled fliers. They glide and climb and wheel effortlessly, never touching each other or the slight waves. Rosa and Jeremy love to watch them. Today, because there is a strong breeze from the northeast the swallows are enjoying the hunt more than usually. Rosa claps her hands at their skill. Jeremy laughs, "That guy with the plane should have spent more time watching the swallows. They never let their wings get into the surf. Even when they touch the water with their bills, their wings stay up and dry."

CHAPTER 15

▼

The explosive arrival of the pilot stirred in Mari Estrella a professional obsession to get to the bottom of the story, to know exactly who the pilot was, to analyze how his appearance reflected the world of narcotrafficking and desde Desdemona's previously unexplored role in it. She thought about exactly how she would go about it. The local news would have covered the cataclysm and the rescue of a mystery man and his parrot, but that was not her genre. The Caribbean regional news would have expanded the crash coverage to include a smug socio-political analysis of how Colombia continued to acquiesce in, if not directly support narcotrafficking which the imperial power to the North both created by its unrestrained consumption and simultaneously made token, military efforts to suppress, but that seemed too glib. The real story, she thought, the big, international story, had something to do with how desde Desdemona's privacy and secrecy in an era of supposed surveillance of everyone and everything had absorbed an obvious international criminal, sheltered him, healed him from his injuries, and held in abeyance a communal decision whether he and his crime should forever remain hidden from view. If told, the story might ruin desde Desdemona. She might compare desde Desdemona to 18th century Australia, or 18th century Georgia in the USA, or French penal colonies in South America. She might question how in a world of interlocking data bases and feverish surveillance and intense international cooperation anyone could ever be hidden. Did it mean that the surveillance was porous, that it was some kind of a joke? She looked out across the reef, watched a pelican dive, and turned to her laptop. She wouldn't write the story and try to sell it to the wire services. Her promise forbade that.

Instead, at most she could work the plane crash and the enigmatic pilot into her incipient novel.

There is something about what I know about the world situation, she thought, that feels like what I know is being controlled and manipulated by the US media, that it's part of some kind of crazy conspiracy. If things were really the way the US media portrays them, the pilot's situation just wouldn't be possible. But here he is. Is this my training and experience in journalism speaking, or does this have something to do with my personal suspiciousness, my constant seeking for things that aren't right and wanting to blow the whistle on them? Is this a chicken and egg issue? Is this really what I think?

*   *   *   *

Bardo eased into the hammock. There was a strong breeze from the northeast, pushing the hammock back and forth. He closed his eyes and focused on what he liked about desde Desdemona. It was again time for his favorite exercise, thinking about purely positive things, enjoying them. He thought about the surf, the palm trees, the reef, the comfort of the hammock, the wonderful food he had eaten for lunch, the joy of having tourists come to relax, the ease and relaxation of the place. He loved the soccer game. True, he thought, I'm getting slower, but the race is not to the swift. The tortoise always wins, as Jimi Hendrix sang, eventually. The rocking and the envelope of purely joyful, happy thoughts lulled him to sleep.

In his dream a huge dragonfly emerged from near the horizon and buzzed toward desde Desdemona. He saw himself standing at a railing watching it sail over the sea, closer and closer. In his dream he thought, "This is an insect, not an airplane. This is a dream." As the dragonfly approached it began to dive toward the sea and buzz and hover just over the peaks of the waves. Suddenly, and quite without warning, a dolphin jumped out of the sea and slapped the dragonfly upward with its tail. Bardo heard the sharp sounding snap of dolphin's wet flesh against insect. At this the dragonfly turned and receded toward the horizon. Bardo awoke. "I'm missing something about the pilot," he said aloud. "I'm definitely missing something." He lay there. The joyful thoughts were nowhere to be found. In Bardo's solar plexus there was a cavern.

The feeling from his discovery that something was missing steadily grew to a sick, tight feeling in his solar plexus. It was familiar to him. Often he awakened from a night's sleep with it. He understood it to mean that he had fallen from radiating with bright, positive joyfulness, and was instead dwelling in dull, negative thoughts of fear or sadness. His initial, habitual thoughts were that these awful feelings had to be escaped, had to be banished, or had to be scrutinized and examined and analyzed and expunged. But that was not what Swamiji had recommended when he raised the issue.

"Do not look deeper into why you have these negative thoughts," Swamiji told him. "It is enough that you have them, that your inner knowing is telling you that you do not like them. Look instead at what you really do want, find out what you really do want. You already know what you don't want from the thoughts."

"How do I get what I really want, assuming I can find out what that is?" Bardo asked earnestly.

The question convulsed Swamiji. His face turned red, his eyes twinkled, and a torrent of squealing, braying laughter thundered from his mouth. "Oh, you must be taking lessons from those disciples of mine! How did you learn to be such a comedian?"

When the laughter had subsided and Swamiji was breathing evenly again, Bardo tried again. "Is there a way to get what I really want?"

Swamiji stared at him. "You're not going to get me started again," he giggled. "You're not going to. I can feel my laughter coming up from my second chakra, but I'm not going to give in to it. You mustn't play this game with me." He giggled, started to turn red, and began to breathe audibly and consciously through his nose toward his stomach, until the inclination toward laughter subsided.

"Did I not tell you to lie in the hammock and turn your thoughts to things that you like? Think more and more thoughts that you like. Don't think about what you don't like. Fill your entire consciousness, your thoughts with things you like. Appreciate what you like. Enjoy what you like. Imagine what you like, imagine it until you can't tell that you're imagining it. This will make you content and happy. You won't care very much about having anything when you learn to dream well. And when you can dream effectively, you get it all anyway but by then that does not even matter."

"I knew it. You don't care if I get what I want," Bardo said earnestly. The comment was too much for Swamiji. "Of course not," he exploded with peals of braying, snorting, uncontrollable laughter. "You're trying to kill me, but it won't work. My disciples have tried this too, but I have practice with this." Then his laughter took over, a whooping, shaking, braying laughter that turned his face and neck red and made tears roll down his face.

*   *   *   *

Ona is standing on the eastern end of Desde Desdemona facing into the wind. She has a large, black plastic garbage bag with her. She is filling it with discarded plastic that has been tossed by the sea onto the beach. She does this once every two weeks. For the past five years the amount of plastic has been approximately constant. Before that, there was very little plastic. Now there are dozens of items, big bottles, ketchup dispensers, small bottles, plastic packaging, tubes from sun screen, bottle caps, shoes, a long list of items simply ejected from ships and villages into the sea, as if it were an enormous dump.

As she picks up the items, she looks at them carefully, then puts them in the bag. Where in the world was this made? Where did it enter the sea? Was it thrown in or did it fall in the sea? While she works, the great mother is present with her, encouraging her, telling her that this picking up must be done. "Where does this come from?" Ona asks.

"Your species makes these items," the mother responds. "These items make the sea sick, and they injure her creatures. When the sea finds a shore, she scoops them up and deposits them on the sand. She says, 'These are yours. Please take them back, I do not want them.' The sea hopes that you will see these things and remove them.

"Thousands of years ago, the sea only had to return to you the bodies of those who had drowned. She did this with vigilance. But now more and more things that do not belong in the sea end up in her, and the sea tries to reject these items.

"When the dolphins first saw plastic, they were amazed. Before that, they knew that all things are impermanent, that they all decay eventually. But the plastic seemed to the dolphins to be eternal. They found it perplexing—it seemed to defy the laws of nature, the law of entropy, the law of decay—but they were not fooled for long. Soon they learned that it was not permanent, only inconceivably slow to degrade."

Ona picks up a motor oil bottle. "Because you pick these up, the sea does not deposit too very much on your shore. She knows in her intelligence that you are receiving her message. Those who do not pick these up, those who persist in dropping them in the sea, receive more and more of these items so that they will eventually be reminded of the sea's concern and displeasure. So they will eventually stop defacing the sea."

When Ona has removed all the items, she takes the bag to the dock. It will be taken on the next boat trip along with the recyclables from the island to a recycling bin 50 miles across the sea to the west. The objects will eventually be turned into building materials and soles for running shoes; a few of the shoes reincarnate. They will eventually be separated from their mates and wash up on the beach at desde Desdemona for a second or even a third time.

*   *   *   *

The pilot shakes Bardo's hammock until Bardo opens only one of his eyes. Bardo is only slightly surprised to find the pilot standing there. He's been expecting this visit for about five days. "I need to talk to you," the pilot whispers. Bardo immediately notices the odor of weed.

Bardo sits up slowly, squinting. He puts on sunglasses and moves slowly to a chair. "I want to ask you some questions," the pilot begins. Bardo nods. He stifles an involuntary yawn. "I am going to be patient and I am going to listen," Bardo chides himself.

"I don't know what to do," the pilot begins. His eyes are darting, and Bardo notices they are red. "I'm obviously in a certain amount of trouble. That much is clear. My family may also be in some very serious trouble because I'm in trouble." He sighs. Bardo nods again.

"If I ask, do you think I will be permitted to stay here?"

Bardo's mind says, "Not if I have anything to say about it, we don't need you to continue to vegetate and be constantly stoned," but his voice says instead, "It is a communal decision, and it's very hard to predict what it will be in your case. There is a lot of sentiment that you have nothing to contribute. At least you haven't contributed anything so far, and there are no apparent prospects. In fact, some people think strongly that your smuggling should be punished." Bardo shrugs. "I can't accurately tell you what people will decide."

"If I ask to leave, where will you take me?"

"Where would you like to be taken? We can take you to most nearby places in the sea plane. We would let you off in the surf and let you wander ashore. You have no papers. You'd be on your own. You could tell people you had wrecked a boat or had been hijacked by pirates. I don't recommend that you mention the plane crash. They would tend to believe a wreck or hijacking. They would probably figure out how to get you home, if that's what you desired."

The pilot looked off in the distance. He began again to try to calculate what he should do. His mind was confused, fuzzy, and far from desde Desdemona. His mind wouldn't respond. It was desperately darting through a maze of streets in Medellin and Bogota and the large, interlocking web of interconnected, dangerous people he had angered. There was no clear destination except escape. But every route was too complicated and dangerous to imagine after the first step or two. And he was nagged and harried by the cheapness of all life there. This was clearly not anything he could think about. Fear was squashing his brain. It wouldn't think. It was stuck. He thanked Bardo in a distracted mumble and walked down the beach completely preoccupied and pursued relentlessly by fear and insect swarms of paranoia.

"The weed was helping me at one point," he thought. "It's free here. Anybody who wants it can have it. It helped me relax. But right now it doesn't work any more. Maybe I smoke too much. Things are too tense and it's not loosening them up. Maybe I need to smoke more."

On the horizon he saw what he thought might be an airplane. He stared at it. His mind stalled. He could feel his heart pounding. His legs were unsteady. He sat quickly under a palm tree, held his head in his hands, and sobbed. "I'm losing it," he thought. "I'm definitely losing it." His body was covered in a cold sweat. His mind was on tilt. So was his body. He sat and shook and sobbed until no more sounds could emerge from his dry throat.

CHAPTER 16

▼

Marley realized something had happened when his foot reached the third rung of the ladder to his home. The music seemed particularly loud, and the place was throbbing with the bass. In the middle of the deck, he found Mari dancing in circles, jumping up and down, totally exuberant. "I have great news," she shouted. "Great news!" She is jumping up and down in place, shaking the floor, cheering and screaming.

Marley couldn't imagine what it was. He had anticipated nothing; there had been not a hint. "Look," she shouted. She pulled from under her shirt a letter and a check and thrust them in his face. "I sold a book. Isn't it amazing?" It made no sense at all to Marley; he thought that she was working on the novel, and particularly on weaving the pilot and the plane crash into the plot. "What book?"

"It's—I know you're not going to believe this—it's a bodice ripper!" She started again to jump up and down to the music. "Yes, yes, yes," she shouted thrusting her arms in the sky. "I sold a book and I've got a check here for $2,200. I'm now a real hack, and I'm gonna be paid even more for my next one."

Marley is stunned. "I'm afraid to ask what it's about. Does it have anything to do with a former television newsperson who flees to a deserted island in search of true love?" She smiles. His eyes squint, "Am I in this book?"

"Well, to tell the truth, parts of you are in it."

"I can imagine what parts," he grins. "I'm not going to be recognized am I? What's the story about?"

"This is not really a complicated story. A woman falls in love with a man who is not available to her. She ultimately seduces him. It's not really complicated literature. This is also not pornography. It has too much plot. There is more description and more longing, more planning, more surreptitiousness. You know, more adjectives, less one syllable verbs."

"Does anybody flush with pleasure?" Marley blurts out. "Do anybody's nipples rise and her body becomes gooseflesh all over?" He's smiling. "Does anyone pant in anticipation or sigh with ecstasy?" The thought crosses his mind that Mari might not think this parody is terribly funny.

She, however, is fully enjoying both her success and his surprise. "If it's so simple, how come you didn't write it? You couldn't. You need to know how desperately this woman wants this man." She pouts, then laughs out loud. "In fact," she says, "Later on, I'm going to show you the very best part of the story. It involves massage oil and a secret trip to his bedroom. She arouses him from exhausted slumber. I know you are going to enjoy it quite thoroughly. I will make it a surprise for you in the very near future, when you are slumbering exhaustedly."

Marley is thoroughly delighted. He notices that he is quivering with anticipation, that he is palpably excited. He laughs out loud and blushes slightly. He wonders how he can slumber exhaustedly in the next fifteen minutes.

✳ ✳ ✳ ✳

The pilot has failed to show up for meals for two days. He hovers even more remotely on the fringe, standing far apart from everyone else, enveloped in smoke. His clothing is now noticeably dirty, and his beard and hair are even more unkempt. His eyes dart and he stares off in space, and he responds only in monosyllables when spoken to. He keeps away from everyone and to himself. Ona has seen this sort of withdrawal before. After dinner, she takes Rosa by the hand and sets out to find the pilot in the trees near the beach.

She finds him sitting on a log next to the altar to Tara. His back is slumped. His fingers are knotted together in his lap, and his head is tilting toward his chest. Ona and Rosa sit next to him.

"I'm concerned about you," Ona whispers. "You're clearly unhappy and you're not taking care of yourself." He does not respond. "If there is any way we can assist you, I hope you will invite us to do so." She continues to sit silently next to him.

After several silent minutes, Rosa stands up, approaches the pilot, and takes one of his hands in both of hers. He looks at her. She is looking in his eyes, holding his hand. She says nothing. He begins to tremble, first in his jaw, then in his chest and arms, then in his legs. A sob emerges from his mouth. Rosa continues to hold his hand, to wait patiently. At last, he speaks.

The voice is soft and slow. To Ona's suprise, he is not in this moment, intoxicated in the slightest. "I have a little girl much like you in Colombia. She may be in grave danger because I am missing, because the plane and its cargo are missing." He continues to sob. Rosa holds his hands. "For now, you may call me El Pajaro, the bird. It is definitely not a good idea for you or anyone else to know my real name."

"I am having a lot of trouble."

*   *   *   *

"I'm sorry, sir," the woman behind the desk says, "your plane will be at least 20 minutes late." She looks up at Bardo, half expecting complaints, but surprisingly, he is unabashedly delighted. He puts down his bag and stands on the hot tarmac. It is a tiny airport, large enough only for small, two prop airplanes. The two airlines that service the strip seem to have a single employee, and her office is in a shed with louvered windows. Outside the office is a single broken antenna tower and a sign stating that it is two miles to town to the south. Two vans are parked near the sign, waiting for passengers. One is trying to jump start the other with no success.

Bardo has been in Belize for two days of secret meetings with security ministers from neighboring countries. Belize was picked as a site because of its isolation from the media. The participants, especially Bardo, look like typical Eco tourists. They wear T-shirts from Caribbean islands, baseball caps, and Teva sandals. They wear DEET insect repellant, which you can smell near them. The topic of the meeting: what to do about narcotrafficking.

The delay is an opportunity for Bardo to engage in a brief version of his favorite exercise. He begins to think about how wonderful it is to fly in small airplanes over the coast, looking down at the Cayes, seeing the turquoise waters and the patterns made by coral, seaweed, and the sea's variations in depth. He thinks about how much he likes southern Belize, the people he has encountered. He appreciates the story of the Garifuna people, here from St. Vincent over three hundred years ago, escaped slaves who intermarried with the Caribe people and found freedom and preserved their west African culture here. He marvels that just as in most Western countries, the Garifuna men and the Garifuna women have separate languages.

But there is an intrusion, a disturbance in his mind as he walks in circles and curving trajectories on the dusty tarmac, looking out to sea, scanning the forest that runs up to the strip, listening to the sky for the coming airplane. Did he do right in keeping El Pajaro a secret from the ministers? And just why did he do that? There was no agreement with the pilot or with the people in desde Desdemona about this. He can imagine how many secrets they must have kept from him. He thinks about boats from Belize throwing bales of cocaine overboard so that it will arrive on the beaches of southern Yucatan Mexico. They didn't discuss that either. He thinks about the story of how a mayor of a small village and his friends all now live in Europe. Didn't discuss that either. He thinks about the dragonfly and the dolphin, and wonders about the message the dragonfly might be trying to deliver until he hears the sound of its buzz.

He turns his head landward; it is a two-engine Islander flying across the lagoon to land. Bardo walks slowly toward the shed and the plane skids and bounces down the runway. No dolphin swats it from the sky.

*   *   *   *

Oscar is floating on his back, drifting in the sea near the beach. There is no wind; the sea is like a mirror. Oscar's eyes are closed against the bright sun. He hears buzzing and opens his eyes to observe, hovering over him, a large dragonfly. He is delighted by the fantastic color of its wings, the unusual iridescent, shimmering blue and green, the magical transparency of parts of it. He continues to watch it. "What," he wonders, "made you such an unusual, dreamlike mysterious bird, what made you so unexpected, so unordinary? I bet there are those who do not believe you are real. And what messages can someone so foreign to usual experience be carrying?"

Oscar watches the dragonfly dart and hover. Finally, it climbs high in the sky and disappears toward the island. Oscar is left with his wondering. "It's a message of change," he imagines, "It's a message from the spirit world. It will become clear eventually." He falls asleep. In his dream, the world of magic sends messages to the people of desde Desdemona in dreams or by insect and bird and fish messengers. Certain people of the island, who do not usually commune with nature or spirit in this way, receive the messages, translate them with ease and clarity, and deliver the messages personally to the appropriate recipients. "Oh, I would like so much to have someone deliver such a message to me," Oscar sighs. "That would be so exquisite! That would make me so very happy."

CHAPTER 17

▼

Bardo cannot sleep. He paces, then lies down again. He stares at the sky. In the distance on the horizon there are clouds that flash as heat lightning lights them up. Overhead the stars are bright, and he listens to the insect and night sounds. In the distance a howler monkey bellows. The palm trees clatter. In his solar plexus there is again a sensation he labels fear, disturbance, anxiety, stress, worry. He stands up and paces. He stands at the railing. He cannot sleep. What, he wonders, is the problem? He lies down again. He watches the stars. His eyes do not close. He gets up and walks to the railing again. He hears Ona breathing; he does not wake her.

He remembers. In his mind, Swamiji is softly talking to him, telling him that negative emotion is a message, and that you cannot travel from negative emotion to happiness by focusing on negative emotion or analyzing it or thinking about why you have it. No, Swamiji is saying, if you are feeling negativity, you are experiencing contrast, what you don't want. Something is in your consciousness that you do not want. If you find out what you don't want, you can find out what you do want. And then, Swamiji smiles when he says this, put your attention on what you do want, fill your being with the images, words, thoughts, feelings of what you want. Bardo grasps the railing. "I'm pretty stuck," he says. "It's not working for me." He frowns.

His mind is searching for ease. But it's not finding it. Instead, he's finding only fear and worry. He looks out across the dark sea and his eyes wander across the sky. He breathes deeply, searching for the first glimpse of relief. But it is just out of his reach. He thinks, "I will wake Ona," but he discards this idea. "She needs to sleep." "I will wake Swamiji," he thinks. But his mind is racing. "What would I tell Swamiji anyway?"

He imagines waking Swamiji from his meditative sleep at 2:30 am by appearing before him. "Can't sleep?" Swamiji would ask before Bardo can even enter the room. "You are not happy to be awake now? Go and drink water."

"But Swamiji," Bardo would say. "No buts," Swamiji would laugh, "When you arrive here at this hour, you need to drink water. When you drink the water, remember how it used to be rain, how it fell on a roof, and ended up in a barrel. Think about where it was before it fell as rain. Once it was in the clouds. Once it was in the sea. Once it was otter piss." Swamiji begins to wheeze and laugh. "Think about how perfect it is to drink and how perfect all this is. All is well. How can you sleep when there are such wonders?" Swamiji cackles in laughter.

Bardo shrugs. He will not wake Swamiji. He will have a drink of water instead. As he drinks he sees his face in a mirror. He thinks about El Pajaro and his plight. Why, he thinks, is this being so hard for me? The man is a drug trafficker. He's stoned all the time. He probably doesn't belong here. He's contributing nothing. He's a burden. I don't like him. Fine, so what is bothering me?

*   *   *   *

The wind is at Acero's back as he casts the fly across the shallows. He pretends to be fishing for bonefish and tarpon, but the fishing is just the physical activity that fills the time while his mind wanders in spirals. When I was young, Acero thinks, when I was a teenager, even then, I was an idealist. I knew that if the productive apparatus of society were organized the result would be economic justice, freedom, peace, and room for growth. It was so far from the sugar factory and the cane field to the library. But in my heart, in my mind I knew that I wanted the changes a workers' revolution promised, and the promise was so sweet. He smiles. I was in love with it, totally in love. Yes, he thinks, that was my first love, the dream that change would come. He looks at the water. The fly is jerking across the top of the swell, and there are two small needlefish nearby.

I was inspired then, he thinks. I had heroes in many lands who spoke many languages in addition to the rhetoric of revolution. I had heroes in Africa and America and Europe. People who inspired me with their stories. He remembers Gramsci's seizure of the factories in Italy, and la Passionaria, and Lumumba, and the writings of Malraux and dos Passos and Orwell. He remembers the longing, yes, he thinks, it was longing, I wanted the promise so much. He thinks of bus boycotts and lunchroom sit ins in America, of wildcat strikes, of the Wobblies, of the International Brigades. All these people and their ideas are a thick, spicy stew seasoned with his longing. He casts again. The sun is on his neck.

And now, he thinks, now I am fishing. I like fishing. His mind wanders to a row of trucks with cane piled toward the sky, waiting in the sun for the factory to admit them. He remembers the arrival of the police. "We're looking for Acero," the shortest policeman says to the workers. "He's not here," they respond. The workers move closer toward each other, blocking the police. Acero watches from a distance. He sees some drivers picking up pieces of lumber, clubs from the ground. He sees others standing shoulder to shoulder, blocking the police. He sees another police car arrive. It will not do, he thinks, for there to be violence now. We're not ready for that, not yet, he thinks. He runs toward the crowd. The drivers turn and see him coming. The police also see him running toward them. They unholster their pistols. "You were looking for me," Acero shouts. "Here I am!"

The police move towards him. But the drivers will have none of it. They do not know that they are not yet ready. The crowd surges to overwhelm the police and disarm them. The officers retreat to their cars and flee on foot through the dust. The crowd cheers and curses them and throws stones. Acero smiles. He casts toward the needlefish.

That was so sweet, he thinks. The beginning sparks of the San Sebastian Liberation Front. Those people were so brave and so inspiring. They loved the island and the dream as much as I did. And now, he thinks. And now. He casts. There is a vague hunger in him, and disappointment. He notices it as he casts.

*   *   *   *

Once again, John Coltrane Ramirez is furious. "If you're not going to stop him from shooting," he shouts, "at least get out of my way so I can see the shot." He turns, retrieves the ball from inside the net and throws it toward midfield. "Miserable defense," he mutters, "lousy offense, too." He kicks the ground. The tide is lapping at the side of the field, and there is only a one goal deficit. This is nothing new.

He notices El Pajaro standing behind him. He approaches him. "Are you smirking?" he asks, "Are you stoned? Do you think in your stoned way that was funny? I don't think it was funny. Not at all."

"No," El Pajaro sputters. "No. Forgive me for saying so, it's just that the kid is too fast and, well, Bardo can't keep up with him. I'm amazed it doesn't happen more often."

"So you can talk after all," Ramirez sneers. He is still furious about the goal, and the suggestion that his team should be further behind rankles. "So you know how to talk and to play this game after all? I bet you're another stinking, wise ass, know-it-all midfielder. What position do you pretend to play."

"Well, I can play defense," El Pajaro offers. "I can do it well. I played my whole life in Colombia."

"Look," Ramirez says in his most patient, yet most frightening, most menacing voice. "I don't give a damn about narcotrafficking. Or how much you smoke weed. Or who you really are, or why you don't talk to anyone and why you sulk around here, but this team needs some defensive help. You're absolutely not going to play on this team unless you can convince me that you really can play. No kidding around. One mistake, even a small one, and you're gone. I definitely do not want to lose this game. And you definitely don't want to contribute to my losing it. That would be even a bigger problem than any one you have now. Is this perfectly, completely clear?"

El Pajaro, who in the midst of this verbal assault has forgotten that he never asked if he could play, responds, "Just watch me. Next game." He turns and walks away from the field and the rising water.

John Coltrane Ramirez smiles. El Pajaro now seems to him to be bigger and stronger. To Ramirez, with his head finally held high and his broad back straight, El Pajaro has begun to look more like the great sweeper he has been seeking for some time.

"Hey!" Ramirez yells after him. "You better be straight or you definitely don't play." El Pajaro turns, considers making a gesture of contempt, but instead just waves and walks slowly away.

* * * *

Carmen Acero's research has led her to the discovery that the mangrove swallows who live on the north shore are not indigenous to desde Desdemona. They arrived as stowaways on a dugout filled with plants and trees. Their nest, buried in a hole in a tree trunk, was not disturbed when the tree was first dug up by Milagros and Oscar. The swallow parents took the ocean voyage along with their eggs and nest, when Milagros and Saraswati later transported the tree back to desde Desdemona. The swallow couple hatched their eggs in desde Desdemona, and stayed. Their babies remained also. Other swallows, for a reason known only to them, flew across the sea to the island to join the first colonists. Now, to the delight of all who watch them, there is a large population of mangrove swallows.

Carmen Acero watches them fly, little pilot acrobats, who skim the surface of the water, as they bank and climb on the wind. She finds the sitting and watching peaceful and entertaining, and she delights in the solitude of it. How unlike my former, busy life in San Sebastian, she thinks.

There is no real conflict in desde Desdemona, she thinks, no real requirement for heroism, nothing as exciting and as powerful as the forces and contrasts that molded my life in San Sebastian. She notices some sadness about the lack of ongoing, daily struggle, the sudden emergence of a question about the ease of her life. But this feeling is ephemeral, and her mind quickly turns to remember instead the excitement of her first meeting with Manuel Acero.

Carmen's parents owned a sugar plantation and lived in a beautiful house in Johnstown. They were not poor by any means, and they managed to send her off island to the University. During her third year at the University, where she was majoring in Caribbean history, she came home for Christmas break in a state of brittle sadness. She had just broken off yet another relationship with another student, and the looming, but unspoken question of what she would do after graduation was a constant irritant. In her heart, two things were becoming clear. The first was that the injustice and inequality she found in San Sebastian had to be remedied even though her parents owned land. And the second was that she wanted a love as deep and as passionate as she found in the poetry of Neruda, even though references to Chilean Communist poets were not to be made at her parents' dinner table.

Early one evening the week before Christmas, Carmen decided to sit down at a favorite cafe on the central square to drink a coffee, to eavesdrop on others' conversations, and to see if anyone she knew had returned home. She liked the peeling paint and cement columns of the cafe, and the way that vines grew up the side of the building. She liked the potted trees, the palms in the corners. The cafe con leche was strong, and the smell of tobacco and coffee and flowering plants and humidity was sharp, familiar and pleasant. There was always a buzzing among the patrons when the cafe was full, as it was now, and the buzzing today was about the new left wing party and its plan for agrarian reform, for the redistribution of all arable land. The couple behind her were having an argument about it, and several students sitting nearby were praising the idea. She sat near the street, watching the traffic and passersby and listening. No one she knew was there.

She noticed that someone was standing over her. She looked up. A handsome, strong, mustachioed man with wire rim glasses asked if he could join her. He had a cup of coffee in his hand. She noticed a twinkle in his eye. She thought she might recognize him from somewhere, and noticed that she was immediately interested in talking to him. She nodded.

He sat down. The coffee lapped the sides of his cup without spilling. "Are you visiting San Sebastian?" he asked, reaching for the sugar.

She responded that she had been away at University and was home for the holidays.

"My luck is so wonderful," he smiled. "I knew I could not have overlooked anyone as extraordinary as you." He blushed. He extended his hand, "I'm Manuel Acero."

She thought that the blush meant it was the truth. She hoped it did; she liked the blush. "Are you the person these people are talking about?"

"We have the same name, but I hope I am more compassionate and less violent and less impulsive and less reckless that he." He paused before each adjective, thinking about it, measuring it. Then he laughed. "I love this island. That's no secret. But most of what is publicly said about me is propaganda, mine or someone else's."

Carmen could feel her heart pounding. "Do you know the poetry of Neruda?" she asked. It was not a trick question: she wanted confirmation that she was receiving what she wanted.

Manuel looked in her eyes. Another blush emerged on his face. "I would like to read him to you. Can we meet here tomorrow?" He reached out and placed his hand on hers; she did not move away.

CHAPTER 18

▼

The first six times they considered it unusual.

"Wake up, Bardo, wake up." Ona shakes his shoulder. He is lying in the hammock facing away from her.

"What," he says. He is talking in his sleep. His voice is filled with cobwebs.

"Wake up," she continues to shake his shoulder.

"What," he says. This time he is almost conscious. "What?"

"You were buzzing."

"I'm sorry I was snoring," he mumbles. "We've been together for twenty years. I snore. I'm sorry." He tries to roll onto his stomach so he won't snore. The return to his interrupted dream is beckoning to him.

"You were not snoring. I said you were buzzing."

"What is bussing?" He is drifting deeper into the felted cotton chasm, sliding slowly away from her voice.

"Buzzing. You were making a noise. You were buzzing."

"Like a bee?" Now he is finally awake from the shaking. "With my mouth and nose like snoring?" he asks hopefully.

"Not like snoring. It was coming from all of you. You were buzzing."

Bardo sits up. "What?" he says. "Am I doing it now?"

"Of course you're not."

"Of course? Have I ever buzzed before? Has anybody else you know of ever buzzed before. I didn't know I was doing it, if that matters." She can see that the clutch controlling the transmission in his mind is not engaged. He's not entirely sure he likes being told that he is buzzing. He's not entirely sure what he's being told.

"Can you describe for me what you heard or, even better, make the sound I was making?"

Ona looks in his eyes. Maybe, she thinks, he thinks I'm making a joke, that nothing happened, that it's a game. "I'm not making a joke," she says. "This isn't some ruse to wake you up. It sounds like this." She clears her throat and softly makes a hi-pitched buzzing sound. "Bzzzzzzzzzzzzzhsh." It begins with a Spanish "v" sound, slides into an almost dulcet buzz and ends with the shushing of white noise. She smiles. "Like that."

"You're kidding." His eyes are like saucers. She shakes her head. He looks pale.

He gets out of the hammock. He is happy and relieved to have his feet on the floor, to feel the wet breeze blowing across the island, to hear the soft rustling of the plants and the usual insect sounds. The sounds are not accompanied by a new, sibilant, unusual buzzing. He walks in a circle. Ona looks at him. He now looks the same as he did when he went to bed. He gets back in the hammock.

"Let's see if I can go back to sleep. Wake me up if you hear it again." To her amazement, he falls back asleep immediately. She hears his familiar breathing, and soon she stops waiting for the buzz and is herself asleep.

About two hours later, she is awakened again. Bardo's lying on his side. And she hears the sound. Bzzzzzzzzzzsh. She listens to it. It is a pleasant buzz, she thinks, quite unlike anything she has ever heard before. It goes on and on, seamlessly, almost electronically. She has a million questions about it, but the most pressing one seems to be whether the buzz will continue when Bardo is awake.

"Wake up, Bardo. Wake up."

"What?" How, she wonders, can he be so sound asleep. Doesn't he want to know that he's buzzing again?

"Wake up." She shakes his shoulder again.

"Was I doing it again?" he asks from a distant place, far, far away. She notices that the buzz has stopped. "It's ok", she says. He slides again into his cobwebbed world, deep in slumber.

Ona is happy. "All is well," she thinks. Something remarkable is afoot. I can hardly wait for it to reveal itself more completely. I've never heard of anything like this before.

∗   ∗   ∗   ∗

Mari is again skeptical. She watches Marley shed his soccer clothing on the beach and ease himself gently into the sea. "It is much better floating than standing," he assures her. "It's much, much easier for me. Come along." She pulls off her clothing and wades into the sea.

"How do you find the dolphins?" Mari asks. Marley says she should watch. Together they float and swim and tread water until they are about 100 meters from shore. "What we do," Marley says, "is think that we want Lynette to come. We think about how much we like her and how much fun she is. We think about how beautiful she is. Think that we would like her to come and help me heal my soccer injury. And think about why we want her to come. All we do is beam to her our desire to see her. Our desire travels easily through the sea to find her. It doesn't matter whether you say it out loud or think it or dream it or imagine it. Just make it clear that you want her to come to us. Join me in this."

They are silent. Marley floats on his back and closes his eyes. Mari joins him. She can feel the sun waning, but it is still hot. After about 10 minutes, Mari has the thought that perhaps Lynette will not come because it is a soccer injury, or because she is there, or for some other mysterious reason. This incipient thought, however, is quickly dispersed by splashing, whistling, and hooting.

"Ah Lynette, thank you for coming," Marley says aloud. "Meet my friend and lover, Mari." Lynette immediately hugs Marley to her, lifting him slightly out of the sea. She continues to embrace and cuddle him against her, gently stroking him with her flippers, and humming gutturally to him.

As she watches this, Mari's mind is immediately filled with delightful images of her making love with Marley, and a message appears in her mind, "I'm happy you are together with my friend. I am happy that you are happy together." Mari is stunned that such a crystal clear communication from the dolphin has appeared to her. "How do you do that?" Mari thinks.

"How we dolphins do it, my dear, is unimportant. You don't worry about how your computer works or your airplane or your boat, do you? We just do it. Isn't it fun?"

"Yes," Mari thinks. "It is such a surprise. I am delighted to meet you. Do you also do something to heal injuries?"

Marley answers instead of Lynette. "All she does is encourage natural healing. That's what she's doing now. It's not visible to me what she does. I have no idea how she does it. It's her immediate presence that helps. She and her pod have been helping desde Desdemona for as long as I know about."

"Yes," Lynette transmits to Mari, "I just focus on a part of him, the part of him that encourages his perfection to shine and I encourage it. I ignore the thing you are calling an injury." The dolphin message pauses. She claps her flippers, reaching out with her tail to give Mari a playful, yet powerful push. "Not that part of him, not exclusively that part of him, you wonderful one." The dolphin whistles and hoots. "Oh, I can see that you and I will have fun together. You like to play just as we do. His legs will both be fine in a couple of days." At that the dolphin pushes Mari and Marley together, lifts them both out of the water, slides them down her back as if she were a water slide, and swims off. In Mari's mind a message appears, "You must get Marley to show you how we all share dreams." She smiles. She is amazed by how soft the dolphin's skin felt as she slid down her back.

✳   ✳   ✳   ✳

"Do you know the future, Swamiji?" Arjuna asks. Swamiji grasps the arm of his chair.

"Are you going to play that game on me again, that game my disciples are using to try to kill me?" Swamiji's eyes flash. His eyes are popping; his jaw is set. He tries valiantly to hold back the exploding laughter, but it is clear that he cannot contain it. He turns red, then erupts in hissing, cackling, thundering laughter.

"Water. Please give me water," he stammers.

"Oh you evil badmash," Swamiji admonishes him. "You and these others are trying to kill me. I know it. You must not play such pranks on me!" The laugh starts to erupt again, but Swamiji stifles it by smothering it. After a few moments, he is sitting quietly again. His disciples peer at him from behind plants and from behind the door frame.

"Time," Swamiji says, "is something you don't understand. Everything is happening at once. All time is simultaneous. All the nows are tied together, some are caused by other nows, some will cause other nows. All those nows are now. When you think about the past, it's now. When you think about the future, it's now. When you dream, imagine, plan, remember, then it's now. So-called reality is just one of the nows. Now is all that there is, and all the nows are here now. It's all instantaneous and a dream." Swamiji stares in Arjuna's eyes. Arjuna flinches first. When he looks back at Swamiji, he's still staring.

This is more by far than Arjuna wanted to be told. "Well, does anything ever go between the nows?"

Swamiji is smiling. Arjuna is not sure if Swamiji is thinking of a new dietary regimen for him or something else. Arjuna waits, focusing on his breath, assured that Swamiji is not finished with him.

At long last, Swamiji begins to answer. He is grinning. "Only one kind of being can travel in the narrow gaps between the many nows. And that being, the dragon fly, travels from one simultaneous now to another through a corridor of time, and it brings messages and seeds that will grow into events into a now that are needed there. Why are they needed? Because the now the dragon fly is visiting lacks something without which various events and certain information will perhaps not arise. The dragonfly is just planting seeds in all the nows, pollinating or fertilizing them, growing them, nurturing them. Weaving the nows, making ideas, making connections grow and bloom into millions of flowers. That is what dragonflies alone can do, bring causes from one now to another, harvest results from one now and transport them to another, knit seamless interconnectedness, sew the unity and interpenetration of all things in simultaneous time."

The disciples are emerging from behind furniture and doorways as Swamiji speaks this. They are staring at Arjuna, with envy. How, they think, could he receive such an important transmission of knowledge?

"Tell me, Arjuna," Swamiji asks. "Do you understand this?"

Arjuna wishes he could disappear. He gulps. He feels the eyes of the other disciples on his face and back. "Well, Sri Swamiji," he begins. "I don't understand it at all."

At the Swamiji jumps up, claps his hands, and bursts into gales of laughter. "I don't either!" he shouts. "I don't either! All of you, eat nothing but grapes." He explodes into red faced hysterical laughter.

*   *   *   *

It is early morning. As he does every morning, Bardo sits on the floor mat wrapped in a purple striped Mexican blanket to meditate. The meditation is simple. First he prays for all beings to be happy, to be free from suffering, to have equanimity, and to attain spiritual bliss. Then he focuses on his breath. When his thoughts take him away from the breath, he gently returns to the breath.

This morning his mind wanders to El Pajaro. Bardo elects to follow these thoughts briefly. He's a criminal, Bardo thinks. His plane was filled with cocaine. He leaves out the marijuana. Cocaine ruins its consumers and turns the country of its origin into a battleground. Acero is right about all of that and the chain of crime and poverty it perpetuates. It's bad. But here, except for free, casual marijuana use, and in El Pajaro's case, constant smoking of it, there are no other drugs except alcohol. There is certainly no drug trafficking here. And the marijuana is all home grown. Even I smoke some occasionally.

Arjuna was a thief, but that made no difference once he was here. El Pajaro was a drug trafficker, and now he's here. Neither was directly involved in violence. Can I let go of my judgments about who he was so that I can see who he is? Who he is matters, holding onto who he was prevents any discernment of who he is now. Can I find him behind the smoke? Does he emerge from that? This seems to Bardo to make sense.

Bardo then returns to his breath. At the end of the allotted time, he dedicates the merit from his practice to the ocean of merit created by the Buddhas for the enlightenment of all sentient beings.

CHAPTER 19

▼

Acero notices that his mind is more and more often producing thoughts and feelings of his discontentedness. What was before an occasional chimera has evolved into a dominant, recurring thought. And towering over all of the dissatisfaction are his thoughts of martyred Che. The blue water, the beautiful island, the paradise he has found are not a salve. There is an abrasion, a rawness in his thinking, disquiet in his mind. He has not spoken directly to Carmen of it, but he is sure she can see in his distractedness, in his ill disguised preoccupation, that there is already a problem.

Acero has never been to Bolivia, but there is something about Che that is familiar and bothersome. As he stands on the beach, fishing pole in his hand, his mind conjures the Bolivian rainforest vividly. The dense green vegetation, the muddy rivers, the insects, the sounds. And in the midst of this dense, many hued green, he envisions Che, his asthma medicine stockpiled in a cave, resigned from the Cuban government, from the Cuban army, from Cuban citizenship, sitting in the jungle on a stump, talking with his small cadre, smoking a large, double corona cigar. Is he the hunter or the hunted? Is he the invader or the exile? What exactly is he looking for? Is isolation and rootlessness, Acero wonders, the inevitable price for single minded, focused dedication to social justice? Or is it eventual death? Is there something suicidal about being a true revolutionary? About rising above apathy? About feeling called? Is there something insane about believing so completely?

Was it Che's unpremeditated speech arguing that the Russians were no longer revolutionaries, that they had lost their Marxist-Leninist way, and had descended to bureaucratic oppression, that led to his being quarantined? Was that his volcano and evacuation? Was that what ripped him from the stability, if there was any of that, of his former life?

How like me, Acero thinks, how like me. He snorts. Comparing myself to Che, how bizarre, he thinks. I never met the man. He was a saint or a devil before I began. He is still a saint, a martyr of the CIA, of their oppressive evil. Another victim of the dominant Northern empire. He casts again and watches the lure sink and the line pull taught across the waves. The fish ignore his lure. They know he's not really fishing and they have no interest in being used as a distraction.

If it were not for that volcano, Acero thinks, I would be working on my life's work, I would be working on San Sebastian. He casts his line. He notices a bitterness in his mouth. He spits. In the surf very nearby a dolphin jumps. The splash is enormous and drenches Acero. Acero's heart leaps in surprise, as if someone had snuck up behind him and frightened him. When he sees it is a dolphin, and not some enormous sea serpent about to sweep him into the sea and devour him in a single chomp, there is a grin of relief. And delight in surprise. A smile. His mind clears. His heart continues to pound. I'd like to see that again, he thinks. And then there is another, new thought that arises, as if implanted in the cortex of his brain. I'm looking in the wrong place, he thinks, I don't know what the right place is, but I'm looking in the wrong one. Comparison and analysis aren't the road. He squints at the horizon and casts again.

In his mind he is surprised to discover a picture of tall mountains covered by snow and a rope with tiny cloth flags fluttering from it. The flags hang and sway in the breeze. The sky is the brightest blue. There is no humidity. And the sun glints off the distant mountains. It's the Himalayas, he thinks. What in the world is that doing in my head? Acero smiles and returns to his fishing. He is confounded. But there is something in the snow capped mountains unmistakably forecasting relief.

When he returns home, thirsty from the brine, baked by the sun, having worked himself into a grudging acceptance of his feelings of his discontentedness, Carmen is sitting on the deck. She is writing. Her eyes glisten, and her dark, long hair sparkles. She looks up from the laptop and waves for him to come to her. "I found a poem for you today," she smiles. "It is Garcia Lorca's."

Acero frowns. "That is the second martyr today," he says. "I was thinking before about Che. Martyrdom is awful. Think of St. Sebastian," he says.

Carmen breathes deeply. She pauses to think of St. Sebastian as human pin cushion, pierced repeatedly by arrows, and then as an island ripped from the floor of the sea and plunged into molten fire. Then she reads in a slow, steady voice:

"I want neither world nor dream,
sacred voice,
I want my liberty, my human love
in the darkest corner of the wind
no one wants."

She pauses, then reads it again. "Is that not like you?"

Acero walks to her. She stands up. He embraces her. "I have something to tell you," he begins. Carmen holds him tight. "I can't shake San Sebastian," he whispers. "I'm afraid I have to move on from desde Desdemona. Che went to Bolivia. I have to find out where to go. I can't stay here." Carmen holds him. She can feel her fear rising through her legs into her stomach and heart. Her mind fills to overflowing with unarticulable questions.

"It's out then," Acero thinks. "We both need to think about this," he says. "There is no rush. Maybe it's just a feeling that will pass."

*   *   *   *

John Coltrane Ramirez stands over El Pajaro. El Pajaro is flat on his back, his head on the 18 yard line and a grimace contorts his face. "That was wonderful!" Ramirez smiles. "I have been waiting for this for years. You have no idea how happy I am at this moment. You, of course, are going to get carded, probably even sent off when you stand up, but it doesn't matter at all. Finally," Ramirez sermonizes. "Are you all listening to me carefully?" he shouts. "Finally somebody has defended the goal appropriately."

El Parjaro hears this as if it were over a static filled short wave radio, fading in and out, in and out. The sky is green from his perspective, and most of the people look like unfocused, black and white photographs or cut out cardboard. The world is spinning and wobbling off its axis. At last he feels breath coming into his lungs. And he feels others pulling him by his arms and clothing onto a stretcher. He hears Ramirez's voice, "You guys. All of you. Look at this. That was correct. That was what you are supposed to do. It has been decades since anyone did that properly. There is no way he should get a card for it. In my opinion, he should get a medal. A commendation!"

Melvin Gandhi is immediately in the keeper's face, screeching in his high pitched nasal voice. "No, no, no, no, no," he explodes. "That was terribly incorrect. Even in desde Desdemona you cannot, cannot, cannot pull the man down with a block from behind inside the box. It's always been a red card and PK.

Always. Forever since the beginning of time. It was a disgraceful, dangerous, harmful tactic. This is not how soccer is to be played."

Ramirez's voice rises. "Of course, that's so, we all know that's so, but that's not the point. That's not the point at all. I have been the keeper here for what? 24 years now? and that is the first time anyone tried so valiantly, so desperately and so successfully to stop a shot. This was great offensive defense. He should not get a medal. He should get a trophy. No. He should get a knighthood."

Ramirez is thrilled to note that water from the tide has flowed over the end line, so that the game must end for now on that note, before the penalty kick. When it resumes, he thinks, el Pajaro will again defend my goal, and he will inspire me and my team, and the intensity of our playing will be greater, and we will play as if we were gifted with talent and energy. And, Ramirez thinks, there really is something El Pajaro can do that we needed here.

Melvin Gandhi, on the other hand, is distraught. He kicks seawater and sand on Ramirez. "You're old and you're turning into a complete thug. And you're being mean. That's a bad example. Bad sportsmanship! You know what sportsmanship is?" The kick is precisely what is needed to break the tension. Gandhi's teammates all start kicking water at each other and at the opposing team chanting, "Thugs, thugs, thugs."

Nobody points out that kicking water is bad sportsmanship as well. Instead, Ramirez walks off the field still smiling, visions of the impermeable defense filling his thoughts. "Maybe another plane will crash. Maybe this one will have a center midfielder in it," he thinks. "No, better yet, a striker. Maybe someone will now come to rejuvenate our offense. Maybe a cosmonaut will arrive. Maybe…"

*   *   *   *

"What a planet," Arjuna exults. "Look at this beautiful sky. And this sea. And these trees! What an amazing island for me to have!" He is standing knee deep in the sea, facing the shore, where Swamiji is reclining. Swamiji's legs are bent at the knees and crossed. His arms are spread wide on the beach.

"What do you like most about the sea?" Swamiji inquires.

"The coolness. The wetness. The waves. No. The animals that live in it. No. The birds that live over it, and dive in it, and the way it reflects the sun, and the moon. I have an inexhaustible supply of things I like about the sea. I like the way it floats me and rocks me. I have no idea what I like most about it." He kicks the water and watches the splash glisten in the sun and fall on the sand. He sees dimples of wet sand. He kicks again and soaks himself. "I have no idea what the best part is." Water beads on his face and nose, and droplets hang on his hair.

"When you are not standing in it and playing with it, can you close your eyes and imagine it with great and precise detail?" Swamiji asks. "Imagine it so that you remember it deeply, and remember all of the feelings and sensations and textures of it, so that it makes a complete, vivid picture in your head that you can return to over and over and over again? I bet you can't. Not yet. I bet it remains flat and pale and greyish and without the complete breath of God in it in your head. But that will change. Enjoy this sea fully! Enjoy and appreciate it fully. As you do so, soon, very soon the sea in your head will rival this one."

Arjuna shrugs.

"Eat anything you want," Swamiji says. "And as much as you want and as often as you want. Make sure you appreciate each morsel and bite fully. Do that until I tell you otherwise."

"Is this a trick?" Arjuna is suspicious. He has never heard Swamiji give such an instruction before. He has never imagined that Swamiji would issue such a directive. "There must be some sort of trick here," Arjuna protests.

"There always is, you silly man. The trick." Swamiji stops. His face reddens. He begins again, "The trick," but it is too late. He starts to sputter and his laugh begins to erupt. The laugh takes Swamiji over, it is loud, whooping, uncontrolled, an enormous flight of honking geese emerge from his mouth.

"Yes," Swamiji chokes, "There is definitely a trick." His face is red, again armadas of squawking geese emerge from his mouth and nose, and waves of tears swell his eyes. Disciples, summoned by the laughter, emerge from the trees and flow down the beach. Seeing them, Swamiji walks into the sea up to his neck. Slowly his laughter subsides. Only then does he turn and face the shore.

He stands neck deep in water, and he watches as Arjuna, lying on his back, floating on the surf with his eyes closed, bobs toward him. Swamiji can hear him humming. He is quite pleased. Arjuna is happy.

*   *   *   *

Bardo has turned clammy white. "So that's what I sound like." He fumbles for the off button on the cassette recorder. "I'm surprised it does not frighten you," she whispers. "It frightens me. I still can't feel it and I don't hear it when I do it. It's just become a by-product of my existence. I doubt that flies can hear their own buzzing." He walks to the railing. They are silent.

Hovering near an avocado tree heavy with fruit, he sees a dragonfly. He points at it so she will see it. "I have no idea about this."

She places her hand softly on his shoulder. She can feel his tightness, the echos from this new, incipient worry. She can feel in him his neediness, his wish for comfort and relief. "I am sure that all is well here," she says. They are silent. They watch the dragonfly hover and dart, its body neon green, its wings a blur of scaley rainbows. The dragonfly defies the wind and follows its own idiosyncratic course.

"Are you a messenger?" Bardo finally asks it. "Please, tell me what I now need to know." He stares at the insect. Ona is surprised by this. It is usually she who speaks to the insects. The dragonfly rises high and darts upward. It is gone.

"When Kafka got turned into a cockroach," Bardo asks, "Do you think it could have been like this?" He frowns and his eyes crinkle. It is a very weak, cheerless joke. It does not serve to comfort him. He knows that he has not gotten a full answer to his questions.

CHAPTER 20

▼

"I've been thinking—I hope this doesn't sound too self indulgent—but I've been thinking about my life's purpose." Marley is struck by how Mari's eyes flash, her fearlessness at recognizing that a question has arisen for her. He is also struck by the Richter Scale size fear this single fractured sentence has shaken from his chest and solar plexus. All he can do is wait for the aftershocks and the fires to break out.

"Maybe this is coming up because Acero is raising questions about leaving desde Desdemona, and those questions are becoming inquiries for me as well. We came here together." Marley feels his autonomic response to what looks like a five alarm blaze. He realizes that his feet are nailed to the floor and that they are in danger of being left behind when the rest of him runs away.

"I was the first woman journalist ever to be given such important stories, stories like the San Sebastian evacuation." Marley is scalded by her use of the past tense. "So I can understand Acero's desire to continue the struggle, to leave desde Desdemona, to go on following the path he feels so passionate about, the one he followed for years before he got here. For Acero his time here has been an extended vacation, and maybe nothing more." Marley silently and fervently prays that the next word will be "but" but he is filled with dread that it will be the conjunction "and". Time stops still. Marley forgets to inhale.

"Anyway," Mari says. She pauses. She looks deep into his eyes. He realizes he has no idea at all what she is thinking. "Anyway," she says again, "I'm not going back. I think I'd rather make a baby." She is staring into his eyes; he is sure that he is not understanding anything. He senses that his mouth is open but that no sounds are emerging. She continues, "Did I scare you so much you can't do that right now?" She pushes him on the chest. "Did I?"

Marley smiles. "It usually takes 40 weeks."

*　　　　*　　　　*　　　　*

"How funny!" Swamiji claps his hands and sputters. His laugh is definitely coming. Bardo waits for it to arrive. "You didn't want to ask me about the—what did you call it?—buzzing." He can no longer suppress it, the squawking, honking laugh has seized Swamiji. "You're in league with my disciples after all," he sputters. "All of you trying to kill me with these questions and answers." At this he erupts again in flocks of honking.

When the paroxysm has abated, Swamiji continues. "You asked the dragonfly and you said it did not answer you. Very well. But that is not the one to tell you. You cannot ask someone who buzzes about buzzing." Swamiji crosses his eyes and grasps tight to the arms of the chair as he tries to disarm his laugh. "It does one no good to ask the shoemaker for watermelons." He winces at this aphorism and grasps the chair tighter. Slowly and deliberately he breathes deeply. There is a long pause. Bardo listens to the inhale and the exhale. "If you want to know about this, you can wait and it will become clear. Or," at this Swamiji begins to talk rapidly so he can finish talking before he is overtaken by the laughter, "Or ask someone else. Ask Ona. Eat nothing but grapes and water. See what emerges." At this he is convulsed with gales of laughter and his disciples emerge to watch.

Bardo wanders off. He thinks, "Approximately as I expected. More to the process, more to process before it clears." He picks up a bunch of grapes and walks to the beach. He sits on a log before the Tara altar and eats grapes. He will just wait. He is sure it will all eventually become clearer. He certainly hopes so.

*　　　　*　　　　*　　　　*

El Pajaro is panting like a tired dog after a long, hot run. "Something about the diet here is making me slow and out of shape," he gasps to John Coltrane Ramirez. "It's definitely something we all eat."

"You defenders are all alike," Ramirez shouts. "You get slow, you can't keep up, you grab and tear shirts, you foul in the box, you complain that it's food or water or a curse or a hex or voodoo. Or psychological. Or karma. Or worse, spiritual." The ball is far away at the other goal. It is dribbled, juggled, crossed, trapped. "But in your heart, my friend, you know what it really is? It's sad, too. You're just getting old. That and you smoke too much weed. And it's messing up your lungs, not to mention that it makes holes in your aura if not your brain. It makes it like Swiss cheese."

"Not so," El Pajaro shouts. "Not so. My aura? My brain? Are you kidding me? Look at you. You can still jump around in goal like a cricket. And you, forgive me for saying it so indiscreetly, are no kid. Not at all."

"And I eat what you eat. And I drink what you drink. Maybe you're still smoking way too much ganja?" Ramirez watches as a foul is called up field. "Probably still way too much weed. But keepers don't have to run backwards, do we? We just wait for the ball like a spider on its web. It's lots of boredom and a little quick terror. But mostly boredom and waiting. Unlike me, you, forgive me for also being indiscrete, have to run hard, remember? You need clear lungs. And a clear head. Now please move up and mark Ben. He's coming this way too fast."

El Pajaro trots to the right. It is not a sprint, let alone a full run by any standard. It's not even a dog lope. It's a saunter. The long ball lands directly in front of El Pajaro as a large, mop headed teenage striker attempts to sprint onto it. El Pajaro swiftly clears the ball high into the opposing midfield, but before he can follow through, he is run over by the oncoming striker. El Pajaro flies briefly toward the sky, pauses in mid air until gravity has grasped him firmly, and lands hard on his back with a deep, resonant thud that turns his world black.

When he next opens his eyes, he is lying on a cot. Perdido stands on the head rail, and Ona is holding his hand. "You're ok," she says. "Just bruised and knocked out."

"Again. Again. Otra vez. Otra vez," the bird squawks.

"Again?" El Pajaro winces. "Wait." He squints. "Did he get a card?" El Pajaro asks.

"Yes, of course," she responds.

"Again, otra vez," the bird whistles.

El Pajaro has a crooked smile. "I was right. He deserved it. There is something like justice here," he sighs.

"I had decided something before the game, but now I know I want to stay here. I want my family, especially my daughter, to be here with me. I want to stay here.

"Please tell Ramirez that I'm not slowing down at all. And tell him also, I definitely don't smoke too much weed. I have no holes in anything, I'm not like a Swiss cheese. None of me is. Tell Bardo." His eyes close mid sentence, he sighs, and he falls back asleep.

Ona watches his breath deepen. The game, she thinks, is so primitive. And so powerful. Who is to account for why individuals choose to become part of desde Desdemona? It doesn't matter to her that he's committed crimes. She knows it may matter to others. She thinks about the seeds inside a ripe papaya, small black seeds held together by the most fragile membrane. What is the membrane? she wonders.

*   *   *   *

"Of course, Swamiji sent you directly to me for your history project," Melvin Gandhi tells Carmen Acero. "Swamiji does not record events in any linear fashion. He always insists that all time is simultaneous and that all things arise from interdependent causes before they fade away. That should probably be expected from a spiritual teacher, but that isn't at all helpful to a historian, is it?" Melvin sits in the sand rubbing leather food into his soccer cleats. His accent is a legacy from his parents, as is his diminutive stature and his long, dark pony tail. "He probably wanted me to tell you about events surrounding my birth."

Carmen has no idea what he means.

"Originally, my father, Arjuna and my mother, Saraswati, believed that they could not have a child. They hoped to be blessed with pregnancy but that did not happen before their sea journey or after they arrived here. After years, they assumed that they would never have a child, but they never fully accepted that as a fact.

"After my father's blissful spiritual awakening, he began to float in the sea. He would sleep in the waves like Oscar, and he would hum songs, and he would share his dreams and visions with the dolphins. The dolphins began to play with him. They liked to play tricks on him to see if they could make him lose his equanimity. They sometimes pushed him under the water to wake him up. Sometimes they slid him up on the beach. Sometimes they gave him rides. They enjoyed both his joyfulness and testing his temper; he enjoyed their playfulness.

"One day a dolphin told my father that he and Saraswati would have a child as soon as Saraswati and Milagros conducted a welcoming ritual. Arjuna replied to this with skepticism. 'How,' he wondered, 'can this make any real difference? How does a focusing of thoughts through a ritual make any difference?' The dolphins, of course, heard this thought. 'Your thoughts, dear Arjuna,' they replied, 'Your thoughts are the only thing that makes a difference. What you think is what you get. What you think is what you are. Focusing your and Saraswati's thoughts exclusively on the joy a child will be to you and preparing for a child to arrive, setting up the thoughts of how much you will both enjoy the child, and filling yourselves with the beauty and wonder of the conception, the birth, the infancy, and the growth of the child is all important. Imagine yourself as a wonderful father. Imagine Saraswati as a beautiful mother. Live deeply in these thoughts.

"The ideas the dolphins gave him were far from unusual to my father. He had, after all, used the same technique to create his brief, wildly successful career in the paymaster's office of the railroad company. The dolphins reminded him of that, so he imagined and thought and dreamed and believed so often and so thoroughly and with such joy about my arrival and my presence that he soon took for granted that I was coming. He fully enjoyed his thoughts of my impending childhood.

"Meanwhile, Saraswati and Milagros prepared a ritual. They made sacred potions of plants and built a hut on the beach. They spent the nights of the full moon there praying and singing and chanting to the great mother, Tara. If I had been a girl, I would be able to tell you specifically about their activities. But as a man I am not permitted to know them, only that they exist, that they are sacred, and that they found favor with the great Mother.

"I also know that the rituals continued until the turtles came up on the beach to lay their eggs, and that after the eggs were deposited in the sand and buried, Milagros and Saraswati took down the hut, floated the materials from it into the sea, and returned to their former lives. I'm told that for a ritual like that to work, when it is over, it must be forgotten, the participants must not think about it any more. They must not try to continue its work.

"One day, Saraswati approached my father on the beach. 'My love, I have news,' she said. 'Our wish has been granted.' Arjuna hugged her. 'We must make an offering immediately to Tara to show our gratitude.' The offering ended up being the three benches that you see now facing the Tara altar.

"When it was time for me to be born, my mother and father went to the lagoon. This is the same lagoon from which Oscar departed desde Desdemona. It is the door by which we leave and enter. I was born in the water of the lagoon. My birth was underwater, just as was Oscar Sanchez's, and like his, mine was also attended by dolphins, who served as midwives, and by Milagros. I am told by the dolphins that the great mother turtle was nearby and that she delighted in my emergence and the wonderful and skilled assistance the dolphins gave my mother. When I emerged from swimming in the water, wrapped in a cloth, at my mother's breast, Swamiji blessed me by pressing his thumb on my third eye, and by promising to be my godfather."

CHAPTER 21

▼

"I've only got 2 pages this week," Carmen frowns. Her eyes are puffy, and her voice is too soft. "And they're awful. It's not that I am blocked or anything like that. There's just too much uncertainty and confusion in my heart."

Mari eats papaya and lime and listens. Their weekly writing session for the third week in a row has crashed. Mari will not read the latest chapter in her novel, one in which a character a lot like Swamiji has a vision of the Great Mother Tara while he is floating in the sea. Instead of that and a chapter from Carmen about the arrival of the colony of mangrove swallows in desde Desdemona, the hour will go elsewhere. Mari is not completely disappointed. She has a character in her book who is a lot like Manuel, and whatever she hears from Carmen might spur her on in developing her plot.

"This time it began when he started reading from Neruda's memoirs. There is a story about Neruda's withdrawing as the Communist candidate for president of Chile in favor of Salvador Allende. Allende, it seems, was a tireless campaigner, and he had the gift of being able to sleep, hunched over in the back seat of a car, on a moment's notice. When they reached remote villages, Allende would wake, pop out of the back seat, greet the people, and make great speeches. When he left, he would immediately go back to sleep. It was as if all of his consciousness were directed at the election campaign."

"When he read this, Manuel began to cry. He told me, 'Everywhere I go, everything I read, every single thought returns me to it. I am on the shelf. There is nowhere for me to go. I am surplus property. Abandoned treasure. Time has passed me by.' Then he went out in the boat for 4 hours to fish."

Carmen's eyes are moist. "In truth there is nowhere for him to go. It's as if the world revolution has had a reduction in force and his job description has become obsolete. The gringos have won: by invading the Dominican Republic, Grenada, Panama, in Nicaragua, in Chile, and God knows where else." She stops in midthought. "He searches for someplace to go, but ultimately there is nowhere."

The idea sits uncomfortably in Mari's mind. "I'm too young," she thinks. "If I were twenty years older, maybe…" She puts her hand on Carmen's. They are silent. Mari can only offer her ears and her heart.

*   *   *   *

Bardo marvels at his good fortune. He is in El Lay, driving an enormous red, rented convertible for a meeting with the Colombian Ambassador. The object of the meeting is to bring El Pajaro's wife and child quietly, and swiftly to desde Desdemona. But at the moment, the 76 degree weather, the smog, and the bumper to bumper, stopped traffic is its own reward. "How I love Southern California," Bardo thinks. "How can anything be so completely made of recycled plastic." He sits motionless in traffic and stares at what looks to him like the fourth identical strip mall. "This is such a delicious contrast with home. My appreciation for desde Desdemona is boundless." He smiles. Horns are blowing, a rare event for Southern California, and sometimes the starting sound for taunts if not actual fighting or shooting.

He thinks instead of the reef and the surf and Ona lying in a hammock, he places Bob Marley in the CD player and turns up the volume. He begins to think of his joyful decades with Ona, first in the States and then in desde. He remembers how when he first saw her she took his breath away. He thinks not only of making love with her but also of their evenings talking on and on into the night, their passion about fairness and justice. As he notices that thinking of her in this way is familiar and produces the same rich, all consuming excitement, the phone rings.

"Hello," he says absentmindedly. The traffic is still stopped. The sun glints off the cars, and there is a yellow cast from the smog. It is Marley.

"I forgot to ask you when you were leaving," Marley begins, "But would you please go to the bookstore for me?"

Bardo is delighted to get this call. "Now I'm going to discuss world literature while I sit in traffic," he thinks. "What could be more Southern California? For that matter, what could be more desde Desdemona?"

Marley, he immediately reveals, wants to be inspired. And he is adamant that he wants no more books that are lectures masquerading as novels or stories. No. The book must be what Marley calls "real fiction." Not polemic posing as fiction. Not self help posing as fiction. The author should be Caribbean or South American or, if absolutely necessary, perhaps North American. There must absolutely be inspiration in the book. There must be what Marley calls "soul" in the book. The description goes on and on, about how characters should have ideas, and the narration should be interesting, but nothing is concrete. And Marley is asking for nothing specific. He continually alludes the idea that literature is supposed to save civilization, that it is revolutionary in that sense.

"I have no idea of what will meet this request," Bardo says. "You got anything more precise."

"Man, I have been telling you precisely for the last ten minutes. What do you think I have been talking about? You need me to go on even further?"

"You want me to write it or just go to the bookstore?" Bardo laughs.

"Man, everybody on this island is already writing something. All the people here are writing all the time, but where is it? They are sitting at laptops, eating fruits, going on and on, meeting with each other, dreaming it up, talking to themselves, but where is it? The major industry is no longer limited tourism, it's unpublished, unpublishable books. Now you say you're going to write one too. This is no good. I told you what I want. It should be in the stores already. Please, just go there, find it and get it for me. I'll pay you back."

Bardo is intrigued by this. He agrees to stop and look. His mind flips through Vargas Llosa, Jorge Amado, Octavio Paz, Garcia Marquez, on and on. Great stuff, all of which Marley has already devoured. He will look for something Marley will like. He will find something that has humor, too. He loves the idea that literature is revolutionary. He loves the kind of writing Marley wants to read. He has no earthly idea what book Marley wants.

When he hangs up, he is still sitting in traffic in exactly the same spot next to the same mall. Is it the same mall? He wonders if he could write a short novel about desde Desdemona. He wonders how it would be different from Mari's book. The traffic is honking. He thinks about how maybe he could be a character in his own book. Would the readers recognize him or could he remain incognito? Can I be a character in my own book if it's not in the first person? He admits it, he has thought about this before.

These thoughts are interrupted by the resumption of the flow of traffic. In seconds he is driving bumper to bumper at 70 miles an hour as if the traffic jam had been a mirage. Bob Marley loudly urges that he free himself from mental slavery.

I don't think that will be so easy, Bardo thinks, but I like the idea that I might be able to do it.

*   *   *   *

Carmen shares a deep familiarity with Ona, and she loves to work side by side with her. Today they are making salve. Together they have cut all kinds of flowers and leaves and minced them with a heavy steel knife. The plants are buttonwood (cordonsillo), trumpet tree (juarumo), and jackass bitters (mano de l'argato). These they sauté in special virgin olive oil in a large cauldron. Later they will return the flowers and leaves, which have been cooked, to the earth, and will mix the oil, rich from the medicine of the plants, with beeswax, which in turn, will be placed in small jars to cool. Ona knows that many of the little jars will end up in medicine chests in New York, San Francisco, and elsewhere. And that each carries the living legacy of Milagros's trips so long ago to the neighboring islands.

Each jar has a little of Milagros and Oscar in it. A little of the dugout. Arjuna and Saraswati are in it. The dolphins. The Great Mother. Everything is in every jar. Every jar depends for its existence on the existence of everything else. Each jar is magical.

Carmen's questions about when to cut the flowers and plants, how long to cook them, how to mix them, how hot to make the oil, are opportunities for Rosa, who works alongside them, to review information that arose originally in Guyana, where it was given to Milagros by her grandmother, which Milagros brought to desde and in turn gave to Ona, who is giving it piece by remarkable piece to Rosa.

Hanging in the air like the scent of the hot oil, however, is Carmen's discomfort about Manuel. Ona believes in her heart with complete and total conviction that all is truly well. She says that with time and patience the contrast Manuel is experiencing, between what he thinks he wants and what he is doing, will lead inevitably to a decision that will bring Manuel into alignment with his life's purpose. The contrast, Ona says, is to be appreciated as a form of guidance. It is the device by which Manuel will reorient himself and again find his way. It's a kind of map.

"I have not been thinking of it in that way," Carmen says. "To me it has seemed an unresolvable conflict, that he is stuck, and that in truth there is nothing he can do."

Ona touches her gently on the back of her hand. It's a gesture of comfort and understanding. In response, Carmen wonders if she can see the situation as Ona describes it. If she could, that itself might initiate some changes. Carmen wonders how her thoughts might influence events she encounters.

They resume chopping up the plants. Rosa begins humming. The tune goes round and round, punctuated by the sound of the heavy knife on the wooden block, sweetened by the smell of the cooking plants. Rosa imagines her great grandmother making this very medicine.

$$*\qquad*\qquad*\qquad*$$

Bardo is exhausted. The Colombian ambassador's love of complex sentences, embroidering the simplest answer with heap upon heap of additional clauses, a practice he undoubtedly admired when he was decades before a student of Jesuits, has produced in Bardo a tiredness so complete, that he appears to be an animal, much like a lemur, so common in the trees of South America, intent on finding a spot for immediate hibernation. Bardo howls in laughter.

Yes, he can relocate El Pajaro's family to desde Desdemona. The Colombians will help by locating the family, bringing them to a neutral location, providing papers, and forgetting the entire so-called event, which after all did not even occur. It will be no problem in finding and removing these people from Columbia. It is such a problem, the ambassador allows, when aircraft, supposedly Columbian but alas there is no proof of its origin or its ownership, have "difficulties" and are alleged without real proof, and one must remember that proof is the essential issue in these circumstances, to be transporting illegal, controlled substances, of which parenthetically there is also no proof of presence on the aircraft. Bardo's mind has traveled frequently to the idea that this language is somehow cultivated by the lavishness of the rooms where it occurs. But his brain has been kneaded so thoroughly by the Ambassador's circumlocutions that it now resembles scrambled tofu.

He falls asleep with his clothes on atop the hotel's king-size bed. The television is on, and it is screaming about the availability of cheap used cars. Bardo wonders exactly where on the freeway these unsold cars might fit in. Soon he is dreaming. In his dream, he hears splashing coming from the beach, and he hears a voice shouting. He runs through the trees to the beach. When he finally arrives after what seems like miles of slow motion running, he is panting. The full moon is shining on the sea, and he sees a naked man standing in a foot of water pleading with an object and pushing it. He comes closer and sees that there is an enormous tortoise. Its back is covered in sharp, grey barnacles, and the man—is it Oscar Sanchez?—has his hands wrapped in his clothing, and is pushing on the turtle. He shouts for the turtle to go back, to return from the beach to the sea. Oscar cries, "Go back, go back. You'll be grounded. You've got to turn around and go back. You need to return to the sea." Bardo's heart is pounding. "Let me help you," he shouts to Oscar. "Let me help you with this. Everyone can find his correct place. Everyone can always find where he belongs." As soon as these words emerge from Bardo's mouth, Oscar faces him. "Yes," he shouts, as he pushes on the tortoise, "Yes. Help me! Everyone must reach the correct place!" At this the tortoise wheels toward the sea, pushes with her huge legs, and smoothly glides down the beach, disappearing in the surf. The waters part and she is enfolded in them. Oscar falls to his knees in the water. He is panting and sobbing. "Thank goodness you came," he says. Bardo is instantly wide awake. His heart is pounding, and his face is salty and wet. In his mind he holds the words "correct place" tightly, as if relaxing his grip on them will make him forget them.

He turns the bedside lamp on. He is trembling. From inside his briefcase, he retrieves the postcard of a drawing of Green Tara he purchased that afternoon. He places it against the telephone on the night table, sits on the floor, folds his hands in his lap, and looks at her carefully in the bright light. He is trembling so hard that he clenches his jaw. Swamiji, he thinks, does not take telephone calls. He pulls the blanket off the bed, wraps it around himself, sits on the floor shaking, trembling and crying until LA's mid-morning sun, knocking from the maid who wants to know if she can clean the room, and hunger all unite to make him stand up. "I'm listening," he thinks. "I'm listening carefully."

He stands at the window draped in the blanket. The sky is yellow, and below on the freeway the cars are bumper to bumper. He moves very, very slowly. "I'm listening," he says, "I am paying close attention. I'm going to move slowly so that I can pay close attention."

CHAPTER 22

▼

Ona awakes with a start. She sits up in the hammock. She hears Bardo breathing and the usual tapestry of night sounds. There is a sliver of bright moon, and the tide is high. The slightest, wet breeze shuffles the plants. She shakes Bardo.

"It's stopped," she says.

"Hunh?" he answers from hundreds of miles away.

"It's stopped," she says. "Are you awake?"

"No." He rolls over, facing away from her and drawing his knees up. His breathing is heavy, slow, and deep.

"It's stopped," she says, shaking him slightly.

He has fallen back asleep. Ona begins to wonder how the buzzing stopped, when to her surprise, she hears it begin again. Its volume increases until it reaches its former level. She notices that she is neither disappointed nor disturbed by its return. "I suspected," she thinks, "that it was not complete. I'm glad I may have helped it start again." She swiftly falls back asleep.

Soon she is dreaming. In her dream, she hears splashing coming from the beach, and she hears a voice shouting. She runs through the trees to the beach. She is running through the brush. She thinks, "I thought there was a path here. Where did it go?" When she finally arrives after what seems like a blurred, intense sprint, she is panting. The absence of a path is curious to her. The half moon is shining on the sea, and she sees two men standing in a few inches of rapidly receding water. They are pushing something. She comes closer and sees that there is an enormous tortoise. Its back is covered in slick, glossy, green moss that reflects the moonlight. The men—they are Bardo and Oscar Sanchez—are pushing and pulling on the turtle. They plead with the turtle to go back, to return from the rapidly emerging beach to the sea. Oscar, breathing heavily from his exertion, shouts to Bardo, "I hope she won't get stuck. She's so heavy. She needs to go back in the deep water." Ona interrupts them by shouting out, "Leave her alone! The mother knows where she is and she knows exactly what she is doing. Tara is delighted that you have seen her, and that you want to help her with her work. She has elicited your compassion. And she has shown you something you need to know. But now you can stop. All is well. All is well." As soon as these words begin to emerge from Ona's mouth, the men turn toward Ona's voice. Their turning makes them slip and fall down. At this the turtle glides from them and wheels toward the sea. She pushes hard with her huge legs, and she smoothly slides down the wet beach, disappearing in the surf. The waters part and she is enfolded in them. Ona laughs out loud. "Good bye, great one," she shouts, "Come back soon to visit us!"

She approaches the men, who are sitting in the surf. Their chests heave from their exertion. They are panting, and tears of relief roll down their faces. "Thank God she left. She knows where she must go." Bardo says. "Thank you. Thank you." Oscar simply smiles.

When Ona wakes in the morning, she recalls her dream with pleasure. She is thrilled that the Great Mother would appear in her dream life, as she does in her waking one. But she is even happier, in her half awakened state, that she can still hear Bardo snoring and still buzzing strongly.

It is several days later when she remembers that Oscar has appeared to her in her dreams, that he has returned to desde Desdemona as he promised he would. She smiles and hopes that she will see him again.

*   *   *   *

The fishermen have caught virtually no fish in the past three days. The sea is disturbed by a tropical storm that will batter the islands to the north, and the fish have decided that they are no longer hungry. El Pajaro sits in the rear of the dugout. He smokes little cigars and watches the motionless line. There is very little to say. Everyone knows that his family may soon be joining him.

Acero sits at the front of the dugout. He continues to hold El Pajaro at a distance, because he considers involvement with drug trafficking unforgivable. And why should he make believe that this plane was loaded with some other cargo? Or that El Pajaro is a political refugee, someone seeking asylum. And why should desde Desdemona accept the pilot? "If I had someplace else to go," Acero thinks distractedly, "I would be there already." He frowns. He is once again stuck.

"And this guy," Acero thinks, "Is a criminal. He is giving nothing to desde Desdemona, and he's a problem. This guy's primary function is to get knocked out in the game and to smoke all of the ganja. That's a qualification for being here? That's why we should flout international law? This is just an outrage."

"Manuel," El Pajaro asks, "Are you still wishing I and Perdido had drowned?" He stares at Acero.

"I have no complaint with the parrot," Acero says, spitting in the sea. "I just don't think you should be here. I don't think we should offer shelter to narcotrafficantes like you. You were committing a crime when you crashed. And you've done nothing but smoke ganja since you've been here."

"And you don't think you should be here, either," El Pajaro smirks. "I am sure I should be here. And you also."

Acero, expecting a political polemic and spoiling for a fight or at least an opportunity to vent his spleen at his displacement from his island and what he still sees as his life purpose, looks at his static, nylon line and at the horizon. "How so?" he ventures. There is something menacing in the question.

"Look at all the coincidences," El Pajaro begins. "My plane crashes near here, I survive the crash, I survive the sharks, I find dolphins, I get brought to an island that will not extradite me. My injuries get healed. I think about what I can do in my situation. I get to play soccer. I find out that desde Desdemona lives in fairness and justice. I could go on and on. The point is that everybody, including you, can see now that my being here is entirely and perfectly acceptable. Correct. That I belong here in every real sense. Even though it's not entirely fair in your eyes, this is the correct place for me."

"I think you might be in the same boat." El Pajaro laughs. "I'm sounding like Bardo." El Pajaro becomes quiet. Then he begins again.

"Look at you. Virtually like me. Virtually like everybody who ever came here and stayed. Your island blows up, you get arrested, you get saved by Bardo and Marley, you say you want to come here, you and your entire family come here, and your wife and children live well here. Only you are having a problem." El Pajaro casts. "There are no fish today to distract us. And you are not thankful for the way things have unfolded for you or finding joy in your good fortune."

"Well, go on," Acero says after a long silence in which the boat rises and falls, the lines remain unmoved, and the veins in his jaw twitch. El Pajaro starts to light another cigar, but stops. "No. I'm getting too slow in the game. I have to stop smoking even this." He throws the cigar in the sea. "So you are not thankful."

Acero stares at him. El Pajaro sees that Acero's anger is waning, that his mind is churning. He is relieved that for the moment Acero is not wishing him dead and contemplating how personally to bring that about. "If this were a movie or a book," El Pajaro begins, "so that everything that's happened so far in your life up to now was in it, you could write or design the ending of it, right? You could make it end anyway you want to. You could dream up the ending. It could be a tragedy, it could be funny, it could be poignant. But for some reason you're not doing that, and the ending you have so far, where you get stuck thinking you're in the wrong place at the wrong time and can't find a right place and are constantly distracted and troubled, that's not working for you. That movie, if you call it that, ends with you miserable, in the wrong place, at the wrong time, suffering despite being in seeming paradise."

Acero looks at El Pajaro's browned face. El Pajaro's face seems fuller, and his eyes seem shinier. He does not remind Acero of a nearly drowned rat or of the person he wanted to leave in the sea or the person he could have strangled only minutes before. The incongruity strikes Acero hard. He shakes his head.

El Pajaro continues. "So, if you pardon my saying so, you need to re-write the ending. Make it something you might like. And then get moving in that direction." El Pajaro casts. Silence returns. The boat rocks. None of the lines moves. A few minutes pass.

"I hope you will not be insulted, but I am surprised by what you've said," Acero says. "What an unexpected insight you have given me. Thank you." At that he stands up in the boat, pulls off his clothes, and jumps into the water. When his head bobs to the surface, there is the slightest smile at the corner of his mouth. He grasps the stern of the dugout. "Row me home," he says. "Please row me home now. I have an important appointment I must keep."

*   *   *   *

Bardo is up at dawn. Ona sleeps on. The children sleep on. He takes a watermelon out of the cooler and with a heavy knife, splits it length wise. He splits the halves lengthwise, also. Then he cuts the flesh from the rind, slices the flesh into triangular shapes, and slides them all into a deep bowl. "I think I am back to eating this for a while," he thinks. "I need to nourish my clarity. And my sense of humor." He begins to eat the first piece. It is sweet, and the juice drips on his chin. "I like it," he thinks. "And I know it works."

He stands at the rail, eating watermelon, spitting seeds, swallowing seeds, watching the sun rise over the sea. As the first light of the sun hits the deck, he takes off his clothes. He feels the warmth and brightness of the sun on his chest and face and stomach. He recalls a fabled sunburn years ago when he burnt his penis. He smiles. "I think I will enjoy the sun on my body, and I will pay attention this time," he thinks.

He remembers the sunburn. The vast naked beach of Martha's Vineyard. The dunes. The sun. His excitement at the depth and intensity of his love for Ona. The newness of it, his complete delight to sit with her, to talk in the sun about the possibility of their having a child, the delight of their marriage. The way the small joint they smoked transformed the bright sunlight into a rich balm smelling of pina colada juice, and how the space between them was so full of delight. How they sat in the dunes for hours. "The sunburn," he thinks, "that was a surprise. I was so transported." He remembers hitchhiking to Edgartown to eat dinner, and freezing on the hitchhike back, and how he could not sit or stand and how regardless, they decided that the name of the first born might be Benjamin. Or Lucia. Or…He could not remember the other possible names. It had been twenty years.

"I think I will wear no clothing for a while," he thinks. "At least while I am home or on the beach. There is something in me the sun will cultivate in this way. And eating watermelon for a while. It has worked before. I know it will work for me again. That is what helps me see what it is that is arriving in me."

He eats another piece of watermelon. He remembers that it is in the cucumber family. That its sweetness depends on rotation of crops. That the inside heart is the sweetest. That he could never eat cucumbers as 80% of his diet, but that watermelon was his delight, the food that fed his wellness. He remembers that as a child there was only a piece or two at a time. How lucky to have found that in quantity it was magical. He could eat as much as he wanted. He feels his contentedness to eat watermelon and feels the sun's warmth across the front of his body. "I am happy," he thinks. "Something great, something spectacular is coming."

✳   ✳   ✳   ✳

Marley has fallen asleep in the hammock. The book he is reading—it is a collection of essays by Vargas Llosa—is open on his chest. The night sounds surround him, the candle made by filling a half of a coconut shell with wax, flickers in the night breeze. At the table, Mari types into the laptop. She is wearing sweat pants and a soccer jersey. Her mind is far from desde Desdemona. She is in the middle of her new commercial endeavor. This story is a romance set in the midst of a violent, socialist revolution on a Caribbean island. The important female character reminds her of Carmen Acero; the leader of the entrenched, military junta that passes for a government reminds her of Marley's grandfather. When she comes to a place where she can stop—her male hero and Carmen, who have been locked in adjacent jail cells in the city jail, are interrupted in making escape plans by the approaching rattling of the jailer's keys—she saves her work and rewards herself with a small glass of Kahlua. "It is going nicely," she thinks. She notices the excitement inventing the scene has kindled in her.

She sees Marley is sleeping. Tonight, she thinks, is a good opportunity to keep my promise to him. I will bring him seamlessly and joyfully from the depths of his sleep to the deepest sexual release. Just like in my little, published book. I will touch him very deeply. I will become a succubus, she thinks. She smiles at this idea, so powerful, so deeply desired, so demonized. He will love it.

After heating a bottle of massage oil in boiling water until it is slightly warm to her touch, she removes her clothes and covers her hands and body thickly with oil. Marley is by then sleeping on his right side. She reaches under Marley's sheets to gently massage first his lower back, then his upper back, and finally his chest and stomach. She notices as she touches his lower back that his awareness is gently returning to him from far away, and that with his semi-consciousness comes a soft hum of contentedness. The hum grows under her hands gradually into a soft, long "ooh" sound of bliss. When her hand eventually slides down to grasp him, the "ooh" grows into a deep, sigh of joyfully exhaled breathlessness. She kisses his lips deeply. He responds with his lips and tongue and by placing his arm around her waist and drawing her towards him. She rolls him slowly onto his back, straddles him, slides down his stomach, and envelopes him with her glistening body. The sounds of their deep, rhythmic embrace merge with the songs of frogs, lizards, insects, and monkeys until they subside in heavy, dreamless slumber.

CHAPTER 23

▼

"If I'm going to do this," Bardo says, "I'm going to keep it a secret. Do I mean it?" He looks at himself in the mirror. He peers into the brown eyes, he scrutinizes the wrinkles at their edges, the grey hair in his eyebrows, the salt and pepper brillo atop his head, the similar stubble on his face. He is staring into himself. He points a finger at himself. "Yes," he says. "A secret. Not that I'm doing it. But what it's about, no previews, no coming attractions, no talking. No information. No hints or innuendos. Nothing. Silence."

Ona is watching him. "I'm going to do it," he tells her. "Do you want to hear the first part of it?"

"It is just the beginning," he says. "I'm going to meet you in Pizza Bills in the next section. So this is where I begin." He turns on the laptop, clicks up the file, and starts to read to her.

"It was almost 2 am, thirty-five below zero, and we had the munchies. We clung to the sides of buildings until we reached Pizza Bill's. Litton used to work there. We stood at the counter chattering, trying to get our eyes to work and our brains to focus. There was a help wanted sign on the wall, right next to copocollo, mortadella, pepperoni, provalone, ricotta salada. I pointed at it. Behind the counter was the proprietor's wife, the notorious Pizza Betty. She had fired Litton twice. She was less than 5 feet tall and weighed 150 pounds. Her red hair was thinning, and her voice made even the tone deaf wince. "Hello, Litton," she rasps. "You and your little friend (she was talking about me) want something, or you just visiting." "We want a large Hawaiian pizza," he says, "and…" "And?" she asks, eying him hard and moving closer. "And?" "And, myfriendherewant-sthejob," he blurts it out. Betty gives him a wilting look. She doesn't want to deal with Litton or any of his stoned, student cronies. But the shop is empty, and after playing the extended version of twenty questions, she hires me.

"Pizza Bill's didn't pay much, but I had a plan. I was going to make enough money to escape the winter and sit under palm trees at Spring break. And, in the meanwhile, I was going to work in the tropics. Pizza Bill's had three huge pizza ovens that ran constantly at 550 degrees. It was so hot that the front window was always a solid sheet of ice. I wore shorts, a tee shirt and sandals. And I sweated constantly. When it was slow, on the week nights, Betty didn't mind if I played salsa records and read South American novels. I lost all track of Litton. I was immersed in the pizza tropics.

"After four months in the pizza tropics, I received a postcard there from Iquitos, at the start of the Amazon River, a picture of a capuchin monkey. It was from Litton. He had seen Macchu Picchu and he was in love. He was living the real thing. It didn't smell at all like pizza. I taped the card over the pizza oven where I could look at it. And then I cried in despair. I knew I was never going to go. My tropics were just an illusion.

"The shop was empty. My usual salsa was playing. Betty put her thick, freckled hand on my arm. 'Kid,' she scratched, 'You're a student. You've been living in Pizza South America for four months, and I've been right there with you. Nobody else has ever been to such an exotic country. Take the rest of tonight off with pay.'

I left. It was almost 2 am, it was thirty-five below zero. I was going home."

He looks at Ona. "I can't wait for the entrance of the girl from Desdemona," she says. He thinks about Stan Getz and Ipanema. She purses her lips. "This is going to be fiction, right? It's in the first person."

He nods. "You're sure?" she asks. "You're sure?"

✳   ✳   ✳   ✳

"Man, you're doing it too?" Marley asks him. The evidence is convincing. Bardo is sitting at the table with the laptop. He is naked. It is 11 am. He is unshaven. There are empty bowls and coffee cups, and he's staring into space. "I told you, we gotta go back to limited tourism. Stop all of this. No more writing!"

Bardo looks at him from far away. "Something wrong?"

"Oh man," Marley sighs. "You know how many books are being written in desde Desdemona at this instant? At least four. And they're all about desde Desdemona. One or two are non-fiction. Two or three are fiction. And at least one of them is bound to be published because some of these writers can actually write.

And then, man, and then, man are you listening to me, people are going to want to find desde Desdemona again. And then, man, we're going to have a problem. A big problem. A problem we maybe cannot solve. And it's a problem when writing is like some kind of sport."

Bardo thinks, "I could put this problem in my book. I could think of a brilliant solution to it."

"And now," Marley continues, "you're probably thinking about how the secrecy of this island fits into the book. Well, it doesn't. The book is incompatible with desde Desdemona. Hear me? Completely, totally, utterly incompatible. It has nothing to do with the book." Marley folds his arms and stares at Bardo.

Bardo's thoughts are scrambled. In one compartment of his brain, Ona is standing in Pizza Bills and there is a riveting magnetism between her and him. There is snow on her coat, and her beauty takes his breath away. He's searching for the words and technique to describe this intense, inexplicable lust at first sight. In another compartment, Carmen's history of desde Desdemona is the center of a critical controversy as to whether it is fiction or nonfiction or, as one wag put it, "Faction." In another compartment, Mari's novel is being gobbled up in airports. Men were benefitted by Mari's resurrection in her bodice ripper of the succubus. Her new novel is having similar, but more widespread effect. "But," his mind counts, "that's only three. Is Acero writing a memoir? That could be the million seller. That could be the real problem. He's bigger than Rush Limbaugh. At least here he is."

"Man?" Marley interrupts. "You understand me? We need to have a meeting with Mari, Acero, Carmen and you. And we need it now. Get dressed. Get shaved. In an hour. This has got to be dealt with. It really has to be handled."

✳   ✳   ✳   ✳

Manuel Acero is not fishing today. Instead, he is walking round and round and round on the beach. He is alone. He is thinking about Mandela's memoir. How it is more political than personal. How the parts he wanted to know are missing. The parts about love, longing, fear, and doubt. He is thinking that he has an enormous advantage: he has always deeply loved the poets, and his language, Spanish, is magical and evocative, and he knows that the personal story is always the important one. Politics fade and change, but the soul is eternal, and the soul's story is the one worth telling. He will tell of the start of his movement, how it became interwoven with his love of Carmen. He will reveal his deep love for her, for his ideals, for his nation, for justice and truth. He will tell the truth about his moments of despair. He will inspire others. He will lift others up. That, he thinks, is what I will do now. I will tell others a true story that will inspire them.

As he paces in circles, he recalls an afternoon conversation in a cafe two weeks after the skirmish at the sugar factory. A student leader and he are drinking cafe con leche at the very back of the cafe. Their table is against the wall. The student leader's eyes jump from side to side, back and forth, scanning the door, scanning the room, looking down at the table. The street is bright; the interior of the cafe is dim. It is hard to recognize faces as people enter the room from the street. Acero realizes after a few minutes that his companion cannot look in Acero's eyes, that there is something too tense, too wary, too tense about his behavior. "There is no need to worry about the police," Acero says to reassure him. "They will not approach us here, though they are always, always watching me." Acero touches the back of his companion's hand. It is clammy with fear.

His companion flinches, and he continues to look down. His eyes continue to shift. "What is wrong?" Acero asks. Then he waits. His companion remains silent. When no answer is forthcoming, Acero leaves coins on the table, and he stands up. "Stay seated," he says. "I am leaving. You must not meet with me until you can be completely at ease when we are together."

When he leaves the cafe, Acero notices to his surprise that no one is following him. The police, he thinks, have begun to infiltrate our movement. Things have become ever so slightly more complicated.

He smiles at the recollection. "I want to tell people about this," he thinks. "Maybe it will help people to recognize what they love and no matter what to pursue it. Even when it seems to be a dream, and dangerous, or just not even to be possible. That's what I want to tell people, it's the pursuit of dreams that counts. Everything else is commentary."

*   *   *   *

"There were only a few people on the island at that point," Carmen explains, "and one of them must have put the Green Tara in Arjuna's altar. We could go through the list of who was here if we wanted to. We could solve the mystery."

Rosa and Ona both smile at her when she airs this reductionist approach.

"Was it one of Swamiji's disciples?" Carmen asks.

"No, it wasn't," Rosa replies immediately. She is beaming. Her response is quick, as if she were playing 20 questions and the item were not vegetable or mineral.

"Is there any mystery in your story of this island?" Ona asks. She speaks slowly and softly. "Is everything fitting together neatly? Is every effect connected to a clear cause? Or are there some parts that still appear to make no sense to you?"

"My research is continuing. There are a slew of questions that I still need answers for. I am looking for them. There are lots of sources I haven't explored yet. I hope I can find the right answers. I know the answers are available."

"What would it be like," Ona asks her, "if the unseen, the unseeable were included in the story of this place. If magic were acknowledged to be—isn't this a funny oxymoron—real. What if there were simply no conventional explanations for some things? What if some things remained purely non-physical, inexplicable and mysterious?"

Carmen frowns. "I was hoping to write a work of non-fiction. I'm afraid now I'm sliding into some other, undefined genre." Her nose wrinkles.

Ona draws her toward her and hugs her close. "Forget about categories," she whispers. "Keep up your work. Everything will become clearer as you go along. In fact, you might want to ask Bardo about Arjuna and the dragonfly. That might help you a great deal with these questions."

CHAPTER 24

▼

Swamiji is floating in the lagoon. His arms are spread wide, and his chest rises and falls with his breath. As he rocks gently on the swell, he feels the warmth of the sun on his face and across his eyes. He hears his breath inhaling and exhaling and the sounds of the stones on the beach as they are raked by the waves. A dolphin circles beneath him, and occasionally gives him a push toward shore. "Your grandmother," Swamiji thinks. "She realized that Oscar belonged to this island even though he had never been here before. How could she know that? I am sure she knew how to make herself available to messages from the unseen presences around her. That is something your species does that only a few of us humans have realized. We don't often make ourselves available to receive the messages from anything. It usually takes us a cataclysm." He yawns in relaxation.

In Swamiji's mind, there appears an image from the depths of the sea. The water is deep blue, dense and cold, and the sunlight is dim. A huge peach colored jelly fish opens and closes its parachute, it shimmers, its tentacles glide slowly back and forth beneath it as it gently rises and climbs. "Oh," Swamiji thinks, "Such a shivery image. How cooling." He enjoys the dance of the jelly fish until it fades. As he opens his eyes, his feet slide on to the beach. He savors the excellence of his floating.

He reaches down to stand himself up with his hand, and he discovers that he is unable to stand up, that his legs are no longer connected to him, that they do not respond to the message his brain sends. He slides his head farther onto the beach and lies there facing the sky. "Impermanence," he thinks. "I need help to stand. I am an old man, and my journey here is entering a new phase." Swamiji closes his eyes. He feels his heart beating steadily in his chest. "I don't think I'm leaving the planet, at least not yet," he thinks. "It is only a new phase for me."

When Swamiji opens his eyes, Bardo's face is blocking the sky. There is concern on his face, a worry that dredges a furrow between his eyebrows and shortens his breath. Bardo is unsure what to say. He just stands there staring into Swamiji's face.

"I need your help to get up," Swamiji says with a smile. "My legs have decided not to obey me." There is no trace of panic in his voice. It is as if he were asking for something as simple as the salt or a glass of water.

"Do you think you can stand after I help you up?"

Bardo puts his arms around Swamiji and pulls him toward standing. Swamiji is much lighter than Bardo expects. But when Swamiji is upright, he does not release Bardo. He continues to clasp his shoulders. He tells Bardo that his legs will still not hold him up, that he needs to sit down. Bardo gently eases him back to sitting on the beach, then he leaves to find others who can help move Swamiji from the beach.

When he returns in only moments with three disciples, all of whom have deep worry and agitation painted across their features, Bardo finds Swamiji slowly walking up the beach. His walk is slow and slightly wobbly. On his face is a smile. A towel is wrapped about his waist. They run to him.

"This is only temporary," Swamiji says to them. "Walking is temporary, not walking is temporary. Everything about me is temporary and moment to moment. I will doubtless call on you for your help in the future. In the meanwhile, know that you are seeing and feeling and experiencing impermanence. You all know the gatha. 'From interdependent causes all things arise, and all things fade away, so teaches the Perfectly Enlightened One.'" He pauses to look into each of their eyes. "Now you can watch as I demonstrate it. And, of course, as you yourselves are doing it more imperceptibly. How I love journeys," he says. "Don't grasp after how I was. Don't grasp for how you thought I would be. The only true fact about the past is that it does not exist now. I have entered a new phase of my journey. Let us celebrate my reaching this milestone, my embarking on this part of my trek."

*   *   *   *

Ona lies on a massage table on the deck. She watches the sky and listens to the sounds of the island, the rattling of the palms in the breeze, the buzzing of the insects. Rosa walks around her. "Am I going clockwise or counter clockwise?" she asks. "Clockwise."

"Could you go in the other direction?" Ona asks after several orbits. "I am sure that will feel much better to me." As she changes direction, Rosa begins to sing or say rhymes in time with her steps. Each has no end. She begins with Life Magazine:
What's Life?
It's a new Magazine.
How much is it?
Twenty-five cents.
I only have ten.
That's life.
What's Life?
Then she sings "This is the song that never ends, it goes on and on my friends," segues after twelve rounds into John Jacob Dingel Heimer Schmidt and Jim Conson from Wisconsin. Ona suggests other endless songs to her. Rosa knows them all. She continues to dance round and round, enjoying infinity.

*   *   *   *

El Pajaro stands in the bow of the boat. The sun is just reaching the distant horizon. His line is taut, the rod is bent in an arc, and the star drag on his reel screams. "It is a huge one," he grunts. "It is running very hard and fast."

Acero stands behind him. He pulls El Pajaro into the seat, and wrestles to pull the harness over his shoulders. "Just hang on to it," he says. "Just hang on."

Every pore in Pajaro's body opens. His arms ache and burn. He forces air into his lungs as if this were child birth. Sweat stings his eyes. Rigor mortis turns his hands to concrete. He clenches his teeth until his jaw throbs. The line, he sees, is running out. Soon there will be no more on the reel. What, he wonders, will happen then? Will it snap? Will the pole be pulled into the sea? The image of a huge fish pulling half a mile of line and a pole through the Caribbean flashes through his mind. "No," he grunts. "You are coming with me!"

The line slacks slightly. El Pajaro reels in hard. "It's still on," Acero tells him. "It's still on." He reels until the line is taut again. Then he holds on and pants until it is time to reel again. Acero, at his request, throws a bucket of sea water over him to cool him off. Eventually, the fish comes alongside the boat. "It's too big," El Pajaro sighs. "We have to tow it in. It will be a huge feast for everyone."

The voyage back to desde Desdemona is brief. Acero's flickering remembrance of Hemmingway's equally gigantic Cuban fish and his problem of bringing it home is dispersed by El Pajaro's questions. "If you won, I mean, if your party won, would your life in San Sebastian have been any better for you after the victory than it is here?"

The boat rocks gently. The sky is perfect in every regard, and there is the softest, most gentle breeze. The huge fish, magnificent in every regard, is tethered to the side of the boat. A more perfect conclusion to a day of fishing is unimaginable. "I wonder," Acero responds after several seconds of silence. "It is the slightest difference, I think, between the taste of fruit and the taste of fruit you have yourself cultivated. Both are quite sweet and very enjoyable. I thank you for asking." Acero smiles; El Pajaro notices that there is an abiding calmness.

$$*\qquad*\qquad*\qquad*$$

"Oh Swamiji," Arjuna is calling in a falsetto stage whisper. It is very early morning. The sun has just peered over the edge of the sea. All of desde Desdemona is still asleep. "Oh Swamiji," Arjuna calls again up the ladder toward Swamiji's dwelling, "I have a small surprise for you. I think you will like it." The falsetto voice brings a grin to Arjuna's face. Swamiji sees him on the walkway, jumping up and down in excitement, beckoning to him. His voice is a sing song, a childlike teasing voice. "I have a surprise for you, Swamiji," he calls. "I think you will like it."

Swamiji climbs down the ladder and walks toward him. "Swamiji," Arjuna calls with excitement, "Are you watching me now?" Swamiji nods. He sits down on the walkway. At this, Arjuna too sits on the walkway, places his legs in the lotus position, folds his hands in his lap, closes his eyes, and disappears.

Swamiji claps his hands and begins to chortle. "Yes. Excellent," he says wheezing and laughing. "Simply excellent! Such a surprise!" In several seconds, Arjuna again appears, again seated on the walkway, before Swamiji. "Did you like that?" he asks.

"This is such an excellent surprise," Swamiji laughs. The laughter fills the walkway and the sky. "Simply excellent. You will probably want to show this to Saraswati. I know she can do this with you. You will probably want to do this together, when it is time for you both to leave your bodies. Go right up through your heads, with the names of god on your lips. This is truly excellent. Keep practicing! Eat fruits, pineapples and mangos and bananas. Drink much water. I know you will be able to do it even more easily than today. I am very happy to see this. Keep on practicing."

Swamiji's laugh has once again summoned his disciples from their sound sleep. He and Arjuna hear the patter of their feet on the walkways as they bump into things and loudly ask each other where Swamiji has gone and begin to search for the guru in an effort to find out why he is laughing. Arjuna again folds his legs in the lotus position, places his hands in his lap, and begins to close his eyes. "Not so fast," says Swamiji to him, laughing and wheezing. "You cannot leave before I do." At that, Swamiji folds his hands and disappears.

Surprised, Arjuna closes his eyes, but nothing happens. Instead, he finds himself surrounded by disciples who interrogate him insistently about where Swamiji is and why he was just laughing. Arjuna wonders if there is room for more than one person to be disappeared at a time, but these thoughts are disrupted by the insistence of the questions.

"I do need practice," Arjuna thinks as he fends off the disciples' questions with a barrage of questions of his own.

CHAPTER 25

▼

The children have decided to welcome El Pajaro's wife and child with the traditional ceremony. They will convey them to desde Desdemona in the century old log canoe originally owned by Oscar and Milagros and rumored to be the vessel they used to flee Guyana. Of course, assent to this is unnecessary: the canoe will end up being the only unoccupied vessel when the sea plane lands. The idea is that if newcomers arrive the same way as the original founders, they have the same connection to desde Desdemona and there is no difference between new arrivals and the original ones except time. And all time is, of course, simultaneous.

When the propellers have stopped and the yellow sea plane has silently glided close to the beach, the rafts, canoes, surfboards, rowboats, and the century old dugout bob at its pontoons. El Pajaro's wife and daughter appear at the door. The wife is young, short, with thick hair and a square body. Her dark eyes are wary. She is wearing a short skirt and stands with stiff nervousness on platform shoes. Her jaw pulses slightly. She does not smile. She is impassive, trying to be strong.

The child has long, thick hair and is shoeless. She is biting on her fingers. Her dress is wrinkled and she carries a pink, plastic satchel.

The adults and children wave and call out, "Welcome, Welcome to desde Desdemonda." The two are silent as the flotilla slowly tows the canoe to the beach. The sun is bright. Both squint; neither returns the smiles. El Pajaro stands apart from the crowd on the beach. He has a bouquet in his arms, and he waves tentatively to the canoe. His nervous discomfort is palpable.

When El Pajaro's wife comes ashore, the children hand her fruit and flowers and grasp her hands to shake them. El Pajaro's daughter stands immediately behind her, within inches, holding her dress tightly with her left hand. As El Pajaro steps forward to welcome them, his daughter immediately releases the skirt and runs toward him. His wife approaches him cautiously, wary, maintaining her distance.

Finally, while his daughter holds him around his legs, El Pajaro hands his wife the bouquet and pulls his wife to him in an awkward hug. She resists, turning slightly away from him. He holds on anyway. He says in her ear that he is really sorry, that they are truly safe here, that all is really going to be all right, that there is nothing to fear now.

Only then does she relent slightly, acquiescing in the hug to the extent of not pulling away. She has not forgiven him. Far from it. A groan emerges from her lips, and her sobs are loud in his ear. He repeats that he is sorry, and continues to hold her. He knows it is just the beginning and that's not enough.

Despite all of this, Rosa somehow convinces Maria, El Pajaro's daughter, to run off with her and the other children, and the small crowd slowly disperses. El Pajaro and his wife climb a walkway toward a house. Snippets of an argument, sharp words but without shouting, including the start of El Pajaro's narration of his ill fated landing in the sea, are swirled aloft by the breeze. No one is listening. All have gone back to living their own lives.

*   *   *   *

It is almost dawn. Bardo sits at the table with the laptop before him, unshaven, wearing a multi-colored hat from Nepal, sweat pants and his favorite ripped African Nations Cup t-shirt. Soon, he thinks, the sun will rise, the household will awaken, everyday consciousness will return, and the story will be put on hold yet again, to be resumed in some other gap between wake and sleep, between everyday life and fantasy. He thinks of TS Eliot, that "between appearance and reality falls the shadow." He thinks about the sutra, that "things are not what they appear, nor are they otherwise." He shakes his head. There is so much happening in every millisecond, and so much to be considered.

The topic, he thinks, is Arjuna. How appropriate. He can hear the palm trees clacking and the waves below him. How, he thinks, can such an improbability be explained. He rubs the palm of his hand across his head. It again feels like the back of an airedale. His hair is again growing in. He makes a note to cut it off soon yet again. Maybe, he thinks, that will stimulate me, open my chakras, bring me the flow of energy so I can explain Arjuna, restore my focus. The horizon is turning pink. Maybe it won't happen, he thinks. Maybe it will have to wait. Maybe my muses and guardian angels are on vacation and out of town. Maybe somebody picked all the thoughts off the thought tree. Quisas, quisas, quisas.

A small dragonfly lands on the top of the screen, its transparent wings held wide, its neon green body shimmering. It startles Bardo. He looks at it closely. "Perfect," he snorts. "Are you carrying a message for me?" he asks. He frowns at it. There is silence. He leans toward the screen so that his eyes are only millimeters from the insect. He stares at it. "OK," he grumbles, "Let's play 20 questions. Are you Arjuna? And are you making me buzz? Is this mischief?" He feels his hands tightening on the edge of the table. "Well?" he demands. The dragonfly walks two strides across the top of the screen and stops motionless. Bardo's nose is 3 milimeters from its wing tip. He stares at it. He imagines that the dragonfly is seeing 6,000 Bardo noses. "Well?" He blows on the dragonfly, but it won't move. He blows again. He gives up. The dragonfly sits on the top of the computer screen; Bardo sits back in his chair and stares at the ceiling. There is a small, brown bat, wrapped in silken wings, hanging from the eves.

"After you showed Swamiji that you could disappear, I know that you continued to practice that 'trick', and that you taught it to Saraswati, and that when the time came for you both to leave the planet, you disappeared together into thin air. Everyone in desde Desdemona still talks about how perfect, how very romantic that was. And how unlike your trip to Trinidad. You both finally planned and executed an excursion perfectly." He looks at the dragonfly, half expecting a smile or a wink, as if to see whether his words are being understood.

"And everyone knows that you and Oscar and Swamiji all talked frequently about coming back. Oscar said he would come back in dreams and he does. Ona has seen him with the great mother. And Swamiji has not left. And you said you would bring messages from dreams to waking, from beyond the seas back to desde Desdemona, from one now to this now." He points at the dragonfly's face. Then he waits. The dragonfly sits motionless on the top of the screen. Bardo thinks of a round clock with hands on which "now" is written wherever a number could be.

"And I suspect that you are now making me buzz intermittently." He pauses. The thought that he is talking to this insect is hardly disquieting to him. He feels a twinge of desperation in his upper arms. "I am not asking that you make the buzz constant. Rather, I would like to know precisely what the message is. More particularly, what is in the present that requires me involuntarily and unconsciously to be an alarm clock? Who am I supposed to be waking up? Myself? Others? And why? What am I supposed to be bringing into now?" He puts his face up close to the dragonfly again. "Well?" he asks. He waits. He expects an answer. What, he thinks, is the dragonfly's voice going to sound like?

Rosa is standing behind him. "Daddy," she interrupts in a voice thick with sleepiness, "What are you doing?" She begins to point at him and laugh out loud. She takes his right hand in both of hers. The dragonfly stirs and flies off, over the railing toward the horizon.

Bardo calls out, "Maybe I will hear it if it is in my dreams or thoughts. Or if you hire a plane to pull it across the sky on a banner. Or if you hire an ad agency. Or a PR firm. Or a team of spin doctors! Try that! Or some billboards!" Rosa continues to giggle. Bardo paces back and forth, back and forth across the deck.

*   *   *   *

Acero's book tour has taken him to a dozen major cities throughout the United States and to various television talk shows. Today he is flying to Pittsburgh. Yesterday, he was in Chicago. He sits in the window seat and tries unsuccessfully to see his reflection in the plexiglass. The appearances for this book tour, he thinks, have a blandness and a uniformity that remind him of fast food. He is unfailingly asked about the beach photographs from Cuba and the videos from the Caribbean Conference in Panama City even though his book has explained that there was no affair, that she was a college friend, that it was, in fact, garden variety, typical US disinformation designed to discredit him. The denial is a source of several mindless minutes for the TV and radio talk show hosts, who then turn to repeatedly and relentlessly asking about various celebrities and what he knows of their real and imagined indiscretions, and questioning him about where he is now living supposedly in seclusion. The latter is a question he steadfastly refuses to answer. Acero wonders if he knew in advance that the overwhelming number of people who would interview him would have read no more of his book than the dust flap and would have heard about him only what the New York Post had once printed on page 6. He wonders if people in the US want to believe that the Caribbean has two parts: one is a large, albeit walled Club Med with razor wire and worth visiting, the other something akin to slums in Calcutta and to be shunned. He winks at the window. He wriggles his mustache. He shrugs.

The commercial aspects of the tour, Acero thinks, have had their benefits. He has made enough money from the book that he can begin a small philanthropy. Every time he appears on a talk show he makes thousands more dollars he does not need. He gives the money to those he admires. And best of all, he is getting paid to listen very carefully to what he is now saying. He notices how his ideas are different from those of the former leader of the SSLF, how he has been seasoned and kneaded and stretched out by desde Desdemona, how he is no longer really a materialist. The unseen and the inexplicable have infiltrated and subverted him, and he's talking about it.

Yesterday, at a Barnes and Noble in Chicago, he cut his finger on a piece of paper. "And so you see what happens when mindfulness is absent?" he said, shaking his hand. "I'm talking about mindfulness," he mutters at the window. Yesterday, when a woman in the audience at his reading asked him what, in addition to writing, he was now doing, Acero responded, "I fish. I see if I can notice and appreciate the perfection in every thing and feel my gratitude. I eat mostly fruit." When the woman follows up by asking what he has learned from fishing, Acero responds, "The key to catching fish is availability. And not gossiping. Gossip drives the fish away. You have to make yourself available to the unseen in life."

"I'm sounding a lot like Swamiji and Arjuna," he mutters in the window. He wiggles his mustache at the window from side to side. He wonders with a grin if he's become a Graucho Marxist.

Acero picks up the skyphone in the seat. He pauses to enjoy the leather of his seat. It is like sitting in a wallet, Acero thinks. It is how a well cared for $100 bill must feel. He dials Bardo's cell phone number. He hears Bardo pick up. Before Bardo can speak, he hears a fragment of Bob Marley singing Revelation.

"I'm in the sky and I was thinking about you. Where are you?" Acero asks.

"In traffic in vast blandness and uniformity. Everything is white Styrofoam, all is clean and regular and normal. I am once again between Malls. I am in Cowlifornia." I don't sound like the Governator, Bardo thinks.

"Still buzzing?"

"Just like a dragonfly. I'm still not sure what the message is. I know it will become clearer."

Acero laughs. "I am sounding a lot like Swamiji and Arjuna and not a lot like Acero in my answers to questions. I'm coming back tomorrow. I've had enough of this for now." He looks for his face in the window. There is a twinkle in his eye. "Let's go fishing."

Bardo pulls onto the breakdown lane. He opens the door and stands on the hot pavement. Acero can hear the traffic and Bob Marley in the background. "Listening?" he asks. "I'm standing outside the car on the Freeway. The sky is yellow. The air smells funny. The noise is constant and mechanical. Everything is made of styrofoam and asphalt. The cars are going 70 miles an hour. But beneath all that is a perfection, a vitality, an abundance, a wellness that is incomprehensibly wonderful and cannot be easily overcome. It is very hard to see it sometimes, but it is definitely here. So-called reality is vastly overrated. So called reality is there just to create contrast. I have nothing to do with the fly paper known as reality except to see it as contrast. To see it as pointing the way to what I really desire. I have to do exclusively with living my dreams. As do you. Tomorrow we will again fish together in the Dream Antilles."

978-0-595-35785-7
0-595-35785-7